THE INCREDIBLE ADVENTU...

THE REINCARN...

VIC MONGOL

by Jerry Gill

Edited by
Keeley Monroy

Ann Darrow Co
Kaneohe, Hawaii

I

VIC: MONGOL

©Copyright 2013, 2015 2017 Jerry Gill
ISNI 0000 0004 5345 9704
Paperback ISBN: 978-1-889823-60-7
Paperback ISBN: 978-1-889823-73-7
Hardback   ISBN: 978-1-889823-58-4
Digital   ISBN: 978-1-889823-40-9
LCCN: 2017904501

Publisher's Cataloging-in-Publication data

Names: Gill, Jerry Wayne, author. | Monroy,
    Keeley, editor.
Title: Vic : Mongol / Jerry Gill ; edited by Keeley
    Monroy.
Series: The Incredible Adventures of Vic Challenger.
Description: "The Reincarnated Cave Girl" | Kaneohe,
    HI: Ann Darrow Co., 2017
Identifiers: ISBN 978-1-889823-60-7 (pbk.) | 978-1-
    889823-58-4 (Hardcover) | 978-1-889823-40-9
    (ebook)
Subjects: LCSH Mongolia--History--20th century–
    Fiction. | Reincarnation--Fiction. | Travel writers–
    Fiction. | Women--Travel--Fiction. | Adventure
    and adventurers--Mongolia--Fiction. | Action and
    adventure fiction. | Historical fiction. | BISAC
    FICTION / Action & Adventure | FICTION /
    Historical
Classification: LCC PS3607.I4355 V53 2017 | DDC
    813.6--dc23

The beautiful symbol on the title page is the word "Mongol" written in Mongolian script. Red, blue, and yellow on the cover are the colors of the Mongolian flag.

Then came the big one. Suddenly, Vic was in total silence and was senseless to physical sensation. The ground billowed they way a sheet on the clothesline ripples in a breeze. The earth lifted beneath her and tilted and just as suddenly it reversed and Vic had the sickening sensation of a sudden fall. Engulfed by hot air and dust, Vic's knees buckled from a sound so violent it made her bones vibrate! Like a flare of lightning the hot memory of her final breath in a cave a thousand generations before seared Vic's brain! Then her world went black!

From Chapter 10

Special appreciation to these super professionals with the Hawaii State Public Library System for helping make Vic: Mongol accurate. You will not find Dulan Bulag on a present day map or earlier maps for that matter. It is now called Dalanzadgad. I searched for days. Finally, I gave in and asked for help from librarians at Hawaii State Library. They could find no reference. They contacted colleagues in Mongolia. They could find no written source so consulted with senior professors who remembered that time and had the answer! Never underestimate a librarian!

Jessica Hogan/Language Literature and History
Marie Claire Hutchinson/E-Reference Librarian
http://hawaii.sdp.sirsi.net/client/default/

Dedicated to
Ashley.
"How's the writing coming?"
&
Hosea
"Hurry and finish the next one so I can read it."

It helped!

Contents

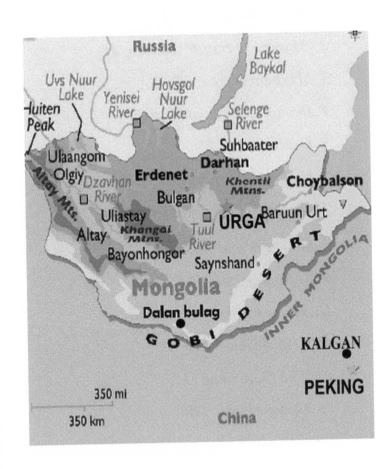

Prologue:

100,000 years ago when life was stupendously savage and every day was a test of your will to live, an epic love was born. Two cave dwellers, Nat-ul, daughter of Tha, and Nu, son of Onu, each a stupendously mighty hunter and warrior to match that time, vowed to love each other as long as the moon would rise in the night sky, which, in their primitive fashion, meant forever. They both died in geologic cataclysms on the very day following their sacred oath. Buried by mountains, one would think their story ended. Yet, since that time the wise of every generation and every culture have proclaimed that true love never dies. There is a reason they say this. In 1896 the moon still rose in the night sky when Nat-ul was reborn as Victoria Custer and as a young woman, the educated Nebraska farm girl vividly recalled her former primeval life and eternal vow. One thousand generations did not cool her love and the recall restored her savage, stone-age instincts and defiant boldness. Now, under the pen name Vic Challenger, she writes adventure travel articles and her work allows her to literally comb the globe in search of present-day Nu. She realizes her quest may take a lifetime and mortal peril may become her incessant companion, but she is determined to do whatever it takes to reunite with her eternal love and time doesn't matter!

In 1919 Vic remembered her primitive past and swore to find Nu. In early 1920, she began her search in Mexico and learned of Stu, a nomadic artist who painted primitive people and fashioned stone-age weapons so might be present-day Nu. By September of that year she was ready to venture out again. Vic and high school friend Lin Li visit Outer Mongolia, an exotic locale with wonderful people, breath-taking scenery, a fabulous array of wildlife and a plethora of ways to die a violent death!

1

VIC: MONGOL

2

Chapter 1

Beats Being Dead!

The wind picked up an hour before sunset. Now it blew a steady forty miles per hour and the rain commenced.

Vic sat in the bedroom turned library absorbed in the latest issue of National Geographic and didn't pay much attention to the rising storm until she heard a loud crash out back. She ran to the back door to see what happened, but the sheets of rain limited visibility to about twenty feet. Vic set to return to her reading when there was another crash and even above the din of the howling wind and pounding rain, she heard the unmistakable sound of breaking glass.

Without hesitation Vic plunged out into the storm and dashed for her hothouse. It took only seconds, but by the time she was inside her cotton day dress was soaked. Halfway down the length of the 100 foot hothouse she immediately saw the broken pane and the tree limb which poked through.   Wind and rain blasted through the breach in the window-glass and whipped her young African coffee trees and hot peppers.

Instantly Vic was back in the tempest, and strained against the wind to make her way to the shed at the far end of the hothouse. When she gripped the handle and pulled, the wind ripped it from her grip and slammed the door against the wall.

A coffee can hung on the wall beside the door and Vic reached into it and pulled out a handful of two-penny nails. She dropped the nails into the large pouch-like pocket of her dress, then took a hammer from the wall and slipped it in with the nails.

Two panels of corrugated sheet tin were on the floor against a wall. One would do the job if there   was no more damage. Vic lifted one and carefully stepped out with the thin edge faced into the wind. When she turned the corner to go back down the side of the hothouse the wind was at her back and it was good for a second. Then a blast jerked the tin sheet broad side to the wind.

Vic didn't lose hold, but tightened her grip and the storm dragged her forward faster then she could step!

The bottom of the tin sheet suddenly whipped upward and Vic found herself two feet off the ground, flying at forty miles an hour! Within a pair of seconds she would either smash against the old elm tree or be raked across her wrought iron fence!

Vic released the tin and one end hit the tree. It spun 360 degrees and the wind held it against the fence. Vic sat up from the three-inch puddle of water she was lying in and checked that the nails and hammer were still with her, then dashed to retrieve the tin.

It was no easier, but Vic learned or perhaps relearned the lesson - a massive result can sometimes derive from meager change or effort. Accordingly, she moved slowly, careful to keep the thin edge into the wind. She backed the tin over the broken pane and held it in place with a shoulder. It was difficult and took longer than expected, but she managed to nail the tin to the frame.

When that task was complete, she headed inside to check her plants, but stopped short outside the front entrance. The hothouse was on level ground but its base was slightly down-slope and water seeped under the door in sheets. Water wouldn't harm the dirt floor, but would make it a muddy mess to work in.

Vic fought her way again to the shed, retrieved a spade, and returned to the front of the hothouse. The wind and rain were unrelenting so it required concentration to stand in place. It was difficult to see through the rain in her eyes, but Vic began to dig a shallow trench across in front of the building to channel the water from the door. Within a few minutes, water no longer came against the front of the hothouse but diverted into the trench and flowed to either side.

She went inside the hothouse to quickly examine the plants and found only a few leaves were lost. Just enough jalapeños were shaken loose for a breakfast scramble. She collected those and headed for the house.

Vic was on the front porch scraping her shoes over the edge to remove the thick mud when a coupe pulled up. It was a friend of her brother Barney bringing him from the train station after a visit with other friends in Lincoln.

Barney shut the automobile door and held his Newsboy cap in place as he dashed for the porch and the coupe chugged away. When he was on the porch, Barney pulled off the cap and shook the water from it.

"Got a nice new wool cap and it is thoroughly soaked! Rain won't shrink it, will it Vic?"

"Well, actually, ...," Vic hesitated to deliver the bad news and Barney looked up, froze and stared.

Not a square inch of Vic lacked a mud pack. He noted the mud coated Mary Jane's and the pouch pocket now ripped by the hammer and nails, and said, "Vic, why didn't you change into work clothes to muck about in the rain?"

Vic's friend from high school, Lin Li, worked part time at Mortimer's Drug and the next day after work she came to visit. The sun was bright, there was no wind and the mud was well on its way to drying out.

Lin greeted Vic, "Wow! Yesterday was wild, wasn't it? Mortimer's closed, and I went home and had a swell time with the family. We all sat in the living room and watched things blow down the street and told stories and drank hot tea and hot chocolate! Bet you were curled up and comfy with a hot cup of fresh coffee and a book, weren't you?"

Vic stared at Lin and answered, "Eventually."

The two went into the library where Vic already had a large map rolled open on the great table bought for this very purpose.

They talked about a planned trip to begin in four days and Vic pointed to a spot on the map labeled *Kalgan* and said, "Here is where I expect we will begin to rough it."

"From what your editor told you," said Lin, "let's hope it really is desolate and we don't meet anyone we don't want to meet. After watching limbs as big as me blow down the street yesterday, I'd like to miss out on those legendary sandstorms we read about, too."

"We'll keep our fingers crossed. I'd like to avoid storms, too," Vic laughed, "but even the best preparation and intentions can be turned topsy-turvy by the unexpected. Remember Burns and the field mouse? From Mr. Gavin's literature class?"

Lin nodded, "Oh, yeah. You mean the best laid plans thing. Well, my guess is, we will get on just fine even when it gets cold as an icicle."

"I'm so glad you are coming, Lin! You are always so positive. It will be such fun to travel together again. Remember how we thought the trip to Chicago was such a big thing?"

"It did seem monumental at the time, didn't it?" said Lin. Vic walked Lin out and watched her crank her Tin Lizzy and drive away.

Their friend Emma painted her Lizzy half green, but Lin's Lizzy was all original black. She did individualize it, however. On the left side of her windshield she painted a red upside down bat, because red is the color of joy and prosperity and general good luck. An upside down bat symbolizes happiness has arrived. Lin wanted to paint two identical bats to double all that it meant, but her mother practically held her hand to insure she instead painted a carp. Lin told everyone it was because she liked to go fishing, but confided to Vic that a carp was a symbol for strength, or persistence, but what her mom really had in mind was 'abundance of children'. "Since mom had six of us and I'm the only one who turned out right, I'm not sure I want an abundance," Lin joked.

After Lin left, Vic lit the gas lamps in the living room and kitchen and prepared dinner for her and her brother.

The next morning, Vic went to her office at the Beatrice Sun to type an article with the recipe for Mayan poc chuc she collected while in Mexico. It was the last of twenty articles she wrote for her column while she was gone. It was almost noon and Vic was about to wind up the day and the week when Jenny from the mail room came in.

"Lots of fan mail, Vic," Jenny said as she dumped a couple dozen letters into Vic's in-box. "Most from here in Nebraska but one from New York."

"Wow!" said Vic, "I love it when someone from way off reads my work, but I hope it's not someone just impressed by the jaguar photo!" Jenny handed her the letter and said, "Open it and see!"

Vic took the letter and slit the top with the opener she personally made - the handle was wrapped with genuine jaguar skin from the Yucatan. She scanned the letter quickly then told Jenny, "It's from a seamstress in New York. Umm, she passed through Nebraska by train returning to New York and picked up a paper. She read my piece about how to make a huipil. She's already made a couple for customers and just wanted to say thank you. That's so nice!"

"That's exciting," said Jenny. "Someone all the way in New York used something you wrote in Nebraska about what you learned in Mexico! No wonder you are always glad when mail comes. Well, back to work."

Vic sorted through the other letters quickly, with the intention to read them when she returned, but one caught her eye. It was from Jason Saxby of Omaha. Although she couldn't quite place it, the name rang a bell so Vic decided to open it.

To Miss Vic Challenger,

I found your address upon recognizing your photo in the newspaper with your article about jaguars and your personal encounter with one. You indeed looked different from the young lady in pink I first met, but I could tell it was you.

I am the boy who tried to take your purse in Omaha and whom you soundly throttled. It was a point of humiliation for a time, to have been bested by a girl, but after I saw the photo and read the story of you and the beast, it became a point of pride.

Thank you for not turning me over to the police and for trusting me to follow your advice. I avoided my promise for two days but on the third my conscience would no longer allow it. Most of those I approached shooed me away but one and then another gave me a project and I always did my best. Without belaboring the details, I now have my own business doing maintenance and cleaning for shops. I have hired five former street acquaintances and we have much brighter futures than was evident a few months ago, all thanks to

9

the throttling and advice you gave me that day.

Unfortunately my long time friend Matt, who was your other attacker, thought it was useless and we parted ways. I thank you for that, as well. Two weeks later he was shot dead in an attempted bank robbery. If not for your direction, I almost certainly would have ended in similar fashion.

If you ever have an office in Omaha, I would be glad to clean it free of charge."

Vic was saddened that his friend came to such an unhappy end, but was thrilled that Jason took her advice and it helped him. When the boy tried to rob Vic in Omaha several months earlier, she didn't realize her advice would be that helpful, but it sounded like Jason had a bright future.

Vic went out to Jenny's desk and asked to use the phone. She telephoned a friend in Omaha who owned a millinery, the source for many of the cloches in Vic's considerable collection. Vic asked her friend to spread the word among other proprietors and suggest Jason Saxby for custodial and maintenance services and vouched for his hard work and honesty. Vic insisted that her name not be used. Then she headed home.

A chum from college drove Barney around that day to visit friends in Beatrice and returned him just before dark. When he came in, Vic told him, "Tonight we are going to be kids!"

"What do you mean?"

"I fried some chicken and roasted us each an ear of corn. I made 3 dozen molasses cookies, large ones. What we don't eat you can take on the train. On the way from the paper I bought us

2 bottles of sarsaparilla each and a box of Crackerjack and fresh butter for the corn."

Vic walked over to a hutch and opened it. She pulled out a box and held it toward Barney. "And tonight you go down in abject defeat, brother!"

Barney laughed and took the box. "At least your imagination is healthy. You know that I am the master!"

Inside the box was the game of Prosperity. It was a Christmas gift to Barney when he was fourteen and Vic was nine. They played more games than they could count, sometimes with their parents and sometimes with friends. Barney won probably 95 percent of all games, everyone else won the other five percent. Vic never won a game. She asked Barney once, while he never helped their dad keep books and she did, and now she had a degree in math, why couldn't she win a game about money? Nevertheless, she always enjoyed games!

That night Vic and Barney, as kids, ate an unnatural dinner and played three long games of Prosperity, all won by Barney. It was near midnight when they headed toward their rooms and Vic told Barney sternly, "This means you owe me another match, you know. So you can't be gone forever. It wouldn't be right to fail to offer me a re-match."

"I can't promise when or where, but I promise you will get a re-match."

"Fair enough, brother." Then they went to their beds and slept well, which is a benefit of kid-ness at any age.

The weekend was a blur. Saturday, Vic prepared for Barney's going away party, then hosted it that night. At the party, everyone ate too much. A friend of Barney's brought his banjo and there was singing for a while. They played charades and friends relived good times from school days. Everyone had a blast!

On Sunday the brother and sister attended church with their parents and Vic cooked a big meal for the family - with unsolicited help from her mother. Then the four went to the pond where their parents watched Vic and Barney compete as who could swing highest before dropping and who could do the fanciest dive. It was an activity they enjoyed since they were children and that is where Vic always shined over anyone and why she didn't mind, too awfully much, losing board games.

At seven Monday morning, Lin pulled up and honked her horn. She drove them to the train station where they had only a few minutes wait before Barney's train departed. Barney promised to send a postcard when he reached Europe and then post a letter from his final stop so Vic and their parents could write him.

When it was time to board Barney hugged Lin and Vic and said, "Off to separate adventures sis. We should have some great stories to share later." Then, where Lin couldn't hear, he wished Vic success on her search. Barney boarded the train just before it began to move and in moments it was lost to sight.

Vic and Lin were quiet during the ride back to Vic's. When they arrived, Lin grabbed her overnight bag from the back seat and went in with Vic. She was staying the day and night with Vic and Emma would pick them up in the morning to drive them to their train.

When they were inside, Lin dropped her bag and stood in front of Vic. "Ok Vic, do something. Say something. You're going to miss Barn and you haven't said a thing about it, not even how glad you are. You know my all-time favorite funny story is your mom telling how Barney helped watch you and when you wouldn't stop crying he stuffed the bottle farther in your mouth to shut you up and choked you. And when he hit you in the head with a baseball. And the time he dropped on you in the pond and nearly drowned you. Say, you're gonna be safer!" Lin laughed.

Vic laughed with her. "I will miss Barney but I'm ok. The part I find unpleasant is uncertainty about when or if he will return. That is annoying!"

A little before lunch time Lin drove them out to Vic's family farm where they were greeted by Terkoz, Vic's gifted wolfhound from her African adventure. Over past weeks, he came to like Lin and especially enjoyed when she scratched his back.

Vic and Lin wore dresses to the farm. Both dresses were light weight and rippled in the gentle Nebraska breeze. Vic's was pastel pink with a white sash and she wore a cloche with pink butterflies on a white background. Lin's tastes leaned to darker colors. She wore a black Paris hat trimmed in red and a small jade turtle was pinned on the front center. Her dress was simple black with dime sized white and red polka dots. Both wore black and white saddle oxfords. Vic sported pink ribbon through her eyelets, tied in a bow and Lin used black and white stripe laces. They both looked decidedly chic.

After a chat with Vic's parents and a good back

13

scratch for Terkoz the two went to Vic's old bedroom where they changed into khaki trousers, shirts and boots, and retrieved several weapons with ammunition. Terkoz lumbered along behind them as they proceeded to the backyard target range, now appearing somewhat less than fashionable.

The range wasn't elaborate but sufficed. With her dad's help, Vic built a simple waist high bench. Twenty five feet out from the bench was a row of four fence posts. To the right end of those posts were two holes, just about a foot apart.

They laid the weapons on the bench and Vic asked, "Which routine do you want to do?" "Toss," replied Lin. "I think just basic," chose Vic. The two developed several practice routines and whenever they came out, each would choose one routine they didn't use on the previous visit. Vic began to load the modern weapons. Lin went to a pile of cans and lumber on the side and took cans to fit on top of each post. She retrieved two planks, each five feet long and six inches wide, and placed them upright in the perfectly sized holes so they stood vertical from the ground. Then Lin used chalk to mark two X's on one board, one a foot above the other. They didn't talk as they set up for they did this often.

After she was kidnapped by slavers in Africa and the gunfight in Mexico, Vic decided it only prudent to keep survival skills sharp for her travels. The question crossed her mind as whether she attracted the brutal encounters. Perhaps the resurgence of her primitive, somewhat savage, instincts attracted similar. She had no sense of how that might happen, but after her recollection in Africa she was open to almost any possibility.

The weapons on the bench were a 12 gauge shotgun known as a trench gun, like Jimmy Jones from Indiana introduced to Vic in Mexico, an old Winchester 73, lever action which belonged to Vic's dad, a .44 revolver and a surplus 9 mm Mauser picked up at the local hardware store. There was also a large modern dagger, plus a stone war ax and stone-tipped spear which Vic fabricated. The weapons were laid out in a row.

When the targets were ready, Vic asked, "Want to go first or shall I?"

"Go ahead," Lin said.

Vic went to the end of the bench to her left. Lin stood quietly a moment then shouted what had become their shorthand for *make a move.*

"Next!"

Vic jerked up the trench gun quickly, smoothly, and fired once. A can spun on its post. As she set the shotgun down with one hand, she lifted the Winchester, cocked it and fired. Another can clanked. So fast and smooth did Vic move that the sound of the rifle yet reverberated when she fired the .44 and made a hole in the next can. The revolver just settled on the table when the Mauser sounded and another can spun. Without slowing, Vic took up and threw the dagger and then the stone tipped spear. Both were buried in one of the upright boards within six inches of an X, which they agreed was acceptable. A split second later, board number two was splintered by the war ax.

"Excellent!" said Lin. "Just about 15 seconds."

"Not bad," Vic said, "but I should be better by now." She went to replace the board she halved

15

with the ax and to retrieve the ax, knife and spear.

Then it was Lin's turn. She repeated Vic's performance in about the same time. Perhaps the only noticeable difference was that she didn't power the ax as much and it hit the board a foot lower than Vic's.

"Wonderful!" Vic told Lin.

Then they prepared again. This time, though, the weapons were all gathered at the right end of the table and Vic stood at the left end. Lin stood with the weapons and talked about her family in China a moment, then mid-sentence, without warning, shouted, "Next!" As fast as she could, Lin threw the ax, the knife and spear in turn and Vic caught and threw each in turn. Next Lin tossed the rifle then the trench gun and with each a can was battered. Last of all, Lin tossed the pistols to Vic. Vic fired the pistols twice each, one shot at a time and every one hit home. As she laid the pistols on the bench, Lin told her, "Perfect."

The targets were all reset and Vic tossed weapons to Lin whose execution was equally perfect.

They then replaced the cans and boards on the pile and gathered the shell casings. "I really don't think we will need weapons," Vic told Lin. "However, my editor's contacts in China tell stories that make it sound like our American West a hundred years ago and after Mexico I will never discount any possibility."

Weapons practice was not their only preparation. Several times a week they did what Vic called loping. They would run slow, run fast, then walk. They would go several miles, going the three speeds in assorted sequences and for various distances. Twice every week they practiced equestrian skill. Basically they took the horses loping and practiced short turns at a full gallop and obstacle jumps.

Vic would always give full effort to her job as a travel writer, but the core motivation for her travels was the search for Nu. She would question people about artists, and observe and sense for a sign of Nu, but she tempered hopes for she was well aware the odds did not favor her.

Beyond the search for Nu, Vic looked forward to photographing beautiful, unspoiled landscape, wildlife and rugged people. Everything she read about Mongolia or heard through her editor promised all of that in spades. Except for a wolf and wapiti, Vic expected to do all of her shooting with her camera but considered it prudent for her and Lin to prepare for unforeseen possibilities.

The two changed back into their dresses and lunched with Vic's parents. During the meal, Vic's mother, Victoria, said, "While you're on the trip I hope you girls don't need to do any of the things you practice. Hope the practice isn't an omen of things to come." After a moment she added, "But then I guess to be over-prepared beats being dead."

Vic and Lin agreed wholeheartedly!

Back at Vic's home they lifted stones for an hour, then practiced with their gear one more time. "It might sound silly," Vic told Lin. "but there may be times when it is beneficial to set up or break down camp quickly or in the dark with no more thought than to tie shoe laces."

Lin replied, "After your mom's observation, I'm willing to practice all you want!"

They carried identical gear. Each had a two

compartment pack with buckle straps on the upper compartment and snaps on the lower. On the bottom were straps to secure their custom pup tents. They re-engineered standard pup tents for this trip. With a standard pup tent, two halves are carried by two soldiers and joined to make one tent for two. Vic and Lin would each have her own tent.

They joined and modified canvases to be one eight foot by six foot piece which required only two poles instead of three. It made for a smaller interior but to Vic the tents had only two purposes - a place to sleep or to get warm, and protection from a sand storm or blizzard.

Vic ordered sheets of MacIntosh material, essentially waterproof blankets they could either wrap up in or use for ground cover and they folded very neatly to take up no more than a third of the upper compartment. The only other item in the top was an over-sized homemade haversack, taken to become extra luggage if needed.

The lower compartment held camera, film, a flashlight and for Vic, a journal also. They carried one extra set of clothing identical to what they would wear - socks, military surplus trousers, and a flannel shirt. Each also carried a down-filled jacket which could be tightly rolled and tied under the lower straps with the tent when not needed. There were no extra boots, just those they would wear, kangaroo leather boots ordered from Australia. So plenty of room remained. Each would carry two items which served Vic well in the Yucatan; tweezers and a waterproof tin of matches, plus a small magnifier and a compass, and Vic carried a pocket watch to keep them on time for rides.

18

After one practice taking their gear apart and putting it back together, they ate a small supper of Vic's locally famous fried chicken with biscuits and gravy, as they recalled good old days in high school. Lin took a fast bath before heading for bed, then Vic laid in a tub of hot bubbles for an hour before she turned in.

By six the next morning they thanked Emma for the ride, boarded, and waved her bye as the train departed Beatrice. It was headed for Omaha where they had an hour wait before boarding the train for San Francisco.

The trip to San Francisco was uneventful but not dull to Vic and Lin. They brought a Sears and Roebuck big book and the pages with women's fashions were ragged by the time they reached the coast. Each made a score of mental notes about what she wanted when they returned. They also looked at homes. Lin wanted to buy a house from Sears like Vic and Barney. Each also brought a book to read and they got off at every stop. They took Oreo Biscuits to snack on and in Denver they managed to wolf down two I-Scream bars each – after having lunch. The train trip was a fun, pocket vacation.

In San Francisco things changed.

VIC; MONGOL

Chapter 2

Murder in San Francisco

Their train arrived in San Francisco on Saturday a bit before noon and their ship was scheduled to embark early Monday morning, so they had a day and a half to be tourists and relax. They left their books and the Sears catalog in the train station for someone else to enjoy and after they registered at their hotel the first order of business was lunch.

After forty minutes of up one street and down another, they settled on an Italian restaurant on the second floor of a building on a short street behind the Embarcadero. There was no view of the bay, but the aromas which emanated from inside were enough to make them forget the view.

After their meal, they went out and stood in front of the restaurant deciding which way to go. They only took half a dozen steps when they heard a woman scream and turned to see a young Chinese woman come from around the side of the building at a dead run. She saw Vic and Lin and dashed to position herself between them. As she did, three scruffy, rough-looking men sprang from around the building. When they saw the other woman, one yelled, "There she is! Get her!"

"Stop! What's going on?" Vic asked, but the men didn't slow or appear to hear. They rushed up to the three women. Lin stepped in front of the girl and the lead man reached out to push her aside. Mistake.

Lin was trained in gung-fu by her uncle Longwei – for over three years now, minimum of an hour each day, seven days a week. The man reached with his right hand and Lin parried, grabbed his wrist, twisted his arm back over his shoulder and took him to the ground and held his arm outstretched with her left hand. She used the palm of her other hand to slam the back of his elbow and it bent unnaturally in the wrong direction. The man screamed in pain and rolled away, then managed to rise and run unsteadily back the way he came.

The second man swung hard at Lin. Lin dodged the fist and the swing went over and beyond her. She stepped into the man, back to him, swung down hard and hit him in the crotch, drove that same elbow into his breast bone and swung up under his chin so hard she could hear his teeth chip. As his head snapped back from that, she used her elbow once more to slam his throat. He stepped back choking and Lin gave a side-kick to his chest. He just sprawled on his back as two more thugs came from around the building.

Vic was learning gung-fu from Lin. True, for only one or two hours, once or twice a week for almost three months, but she was inspired when she saw what Lin did to the two men in less than 10 seconds. She stepped to block the way of the third man and he swung at her. Vic dodged and swung at the man who dodged and swung. Again, Vic dodged and swung at the man who dodged and swung. Then Vic kicked at the man's crotch but he crossed his wrists to block it and kicked at Vic. Vic crossed her wrists and blocked the kick, then stepped sideways and shot a side kick at the man's chest. He turned sideways and let the kick pass. Vic went with the momentum and spun around as the man stepped toward her with a punch that missed.

Vic was irritated. When the man punched at her again, she stepped to the side just enough so he missed, grabbed his arm and used his momentum and her weight, to whirl him around and into the side of the building. Immediately she locked her arm around his neck and spun him around again to ram his head into the wall. He didn't fall so she gripped a shoulder, grasped his hair for leverage and drove his forehead into the wall and then did it again. Then she let go and the man crumpled to the ground unconscious.

When the last two men came on the scene, one grabbed the stranger. The other began a match with Lin which was pretty much a stand off. Vic stepped toward them to help. As she did the man got lucky and Lin moved a bit too slow. A kick intended for her chest clipped her shoulder, but still with enough power to knock Lin down. It surprised Vic when he suddenly spun and slammed the side of her head and sent her sprawling!

Without hesitation he turned back to Lin who was about to rise. He reached behind and from

23

under his jacket he pulled a Bowie knife and drew back to throw!

Vic saw the knife before it was fully out. A small flower bed beside the building was lined with red bricks. As Vic rose, she grabbed a brick and hurled it into the back of the man's head. He bellowed, spun, and snapped the knife! Vic turned sideways just in time and the knife was buried in the plank wall!

That gave Lin time enough to stand, kick the man's groin from behind, and slam her elbow rapid fire three times into his lower spine. The man howled and spun with his arm out to strike Lin but she expected it and dropped. Then the man jammed his hand into a pants pocket and pulled out a Derringer. Vic saw the small pistol coming out and so fast it was a blur she yelled as she pulled the knife from the wall and hurled it underhanded! The man turned toward Vic when she yelled and raised the Derringer but he never fired. His knife went into him just under his ribs, sliced his liver and pierced the lower lobe of his right lung. The man gasped and dropped the weapon as he looked down at the knife. With knees locked he toppled forward like a hewn tree and the weight of his body drove the knife guard through the grisly wound until most of the handle was lodged inside the now dead body.

Instantly, Vic and Lin's attention were drawn to the other woman who struggled against the one remaining man. With two of their band unconscious on the ground, one on the run with a mangled arm and another dead, the one with the girl let her go and ran as soon as he saw Vic and Lin coming.

24

The woman was knocked to the ground but was up in a flash.

"I've got to follow him!" she said in a loud whisper waving them to follow. "I deputize you both!" Then she ran after the last man.

Vic and Lin looked at each other for a second, and then at the crowd already gathered around the men on the ground. "Our adventure may be officially begun," said Vic. "Want to follow?"

"Why not?"Lin said and they ran full steam after the woman, for she was already out of sight. When they came out at the end of the alley, Vic spotted her half a block down the street and they turned after her.

They followed the woman into another alley and found her moving slowly along the brick wall. The alley was a dead end with several doors along both sides. The woman stopped to listen at each door. Lin joined the woman and Vic went to the opposite side of the street to listen at doors. She didn't know what she was listening for, but figured if she heard anything unusual, she would let the stranger know.

When they met at the end, the woman asked Vic, "Did you hear anything?"

Vic shook her head then said, "Why don't you tell us what this is all about."

"Yeah," said Lin. "We killed a guy back there. We could go to prison. Are we really deputies? You're not a crook are you? Those weren't policemen?"

"Police? No. Definitely not! I'm Evelyn Chan. I'm a detective." Enthusiastically she shook hands with them and thanked them for the help. "I guess you aren't legally deputies but I know people at police headquarters so you are OK."

"Your gung-fu is swell, I wish I could do what you did" she told Lin with a big smile, then looked at Vic and said, "You're gung-fu isn't so good but you seem to be a tough nut." Vic and Lin both laughed and thanked her for the compliments.

Then Lin pressed Evelyn to explain. Evelyn asked where they lived and they told her they were visitors. They began to walk toward the hotel as Evelyn told her story.

First she assured them not to worry about prison. "I was in danger and you helped. He died by his own weapon. If he hadn't pulled those weapons he wouldn't be dead.

"So you are with the police?" Vic asked.

"No. I'm a private detective."

"But you work with the police?" Vic asked.

"You look kind of young for a private detective," Lin said.

Evelyn looked a little sheepish as they walked on. "Well I don't work with the police", she emphasized WITH. "But when I solve this case I could contact them. Several inspectors know my uncle and that would make everything OK."

"Is your uncle on the police force?" Vic asked.

"Not here. He's a detective in the Honolulu Police Department in Hawaii. But he has helped the police here on cases and they know him well." Evelyn's pride and enthusiasm were both evident.

By then they were back at the hotel so they went out on the coffee shop veranda. Lin and Evelyn ordered tea and Vic drank coffee and Evelyn continued the story.

A local dowager, Miss Ernestine Gage, planned a house party for the weekend at her

26

estate just outside the city. In attendance were a great nephew and his wife, a third cousin and her husband, and a niece Cora with her fiancé, plus three servants, an attorney and Evelyn. Evelyn was invited by Cora and her fiancé Seth.

Miss Gage was a blunt, to the point person. She let it be known that she was unhappy with some of her potential heirs and called them together to give new instructions to her attorney, in their presence and explain why. Evelyn knew Cora on a casual basis. They met each other at another party and a couple of times for lunch. Cora knew Evelyn was a detective and knew her uncle's reputation so she confided in Evelyn that she heard two of the other heirs make threats toward her aunt and when she told her fiancé, Seth, he insisted they invite Evelyn to attend the weekend get-together. He convinced Cora that with an attorney and detective both in attendance, tempers might be managed better.

Evelyn gladly accepted the invitation even though at the time she felt there was probably no reason for Cora to worry. After all, wills are changed every day, and people threaten people every day but there is no epidemic of murders. She thought it would be valuable experience, though, and it might serve as a preventive measure. It didn't.

Evelyn arrived at the estate late afternoon Friday with Cora and Seth. The others were already there. Cora informed Miss Gage earlier that Evelyn would attend and why, so as soon as they arrived, Miss Gage took Evelyn into the library and spoke with her privately. She told Evelyn that she felt she was in no danger because she thought the whole bunch except for Cora

27

wouldn't have the backbone to carry out the threats, and Cora was the only one she trusted. Even so, Miss Gage said Evelyn was welcome to stay the weekend. She also told Evelyn she might hire her for further work after the weekend but didn't elaborate.

Then on condition of secrecy, she confided in Evelyn that only one change would be made to her will, but she wished all involved to know why. She especially wanted those who would benefit to know that it was not because of any goodness on their part.

Then Miss Gage leaned to Evelyn and whispered that her physician said her heart was bad and predicted she would not see Christmas, only 100 days away, so there was no time to lose. She wished a friendly dinner and in the morning, she would share her plan with the group, then she and her attorney would go into her study, draw up the will and she would sign it right there and then. As they left the room, Miss Gage whispered, "I hope I'll be forgiven."

"It made me sad to hear she had so little time," Evelyn told Vic and Lin. "She reminded me of my grandmother except not Chinese, of course. She was a sweet lady."

"So what happened?" Lin asked.

They were only served a first course of thick beef stew and cowboy toast. Shortly after the stew was served it happened. Miss Gage looked startled and put her hand on her upper chest and in a raspy voice told the butler to call her physician. She wheezed and scratched at her throat, then began to thrash and fell out of her chair. Seth picked up Miss Gage and laid her on the settee in the room. The maid brought smelling salts, but it was no good. She was gone. Cora and the maid cried. "The others seemed upset but not overly so, and they all eyed one another accusingly.

"Why were you following those men? Why did they grab you? Was their attack related to this?" Vic asked.

"It must be," Evelyn told them. "I'm not on any other case, but I wasn't following them."

"What were you doing when they grabbed you?" asked Lin.

"I was following the suspects. All of them! I couldn't believe it when both couples came down here together!"

"Four suspects?" asked Vic. "Aren't there six, even if you don't count the servants?"

"And didn't she have a heart attack?" asked Lin. "Wasn't it just someone's good luck that she died?"

Evelyn didn't think so. "I had a cousin die from a heart attack a couple of years back. I didn't see it but I've heard the story at least a dozen times. He grabbed at his heart. He got pale. He grabbed his left arm. He sighed and his eyes rolled back in his head and he fell down, deader than a doornail. That doesn't sound anything like Miss Gage. She scratched at her upper chest, and her voice was raspy and she couldn't breathe. Her physician was surprised, too. He first told her a month ago, but just saw her and confirmed the bad news last week. He really thought she might have three months or more. Those circumstances plus the social situation smells like sour mackerel in my book. I'm working alone so I thought I would just tail one couple to see if I could learn something or at least rule out someone. It was a surprise when four of them came together down on the Embarcadero. I was a block from them when they went into a building and that was when those guys tried to grab me!"

Then Evelyn nodded at Vic, "You're right, Vic, there are six suspects. I can't let my personal thoughts interfere. Uncle Charlie has told me that often. Except he says, *Even most gentle puppy will bite most kind master if have rabies. Chance at easy money like rabies to greedy person.*"

Evelyn looked over at Lin and said, "You look so young and sweet, Lin, but your gung-fu is brutal! I heard that guy's arm rip!"

"Uncle Longwei says you should only fight to defend yourself and your family, but be brutal and finish each enemy quickly in case more come."

Evelyn said, "That lesson came in handy today! There was another and then another! Thanks again for coming to my rescue! I'm pretty sure they planned to kill me."

It took little persuasion for Evelyn to enlist Vic and Lin on the case as both were totally intrigued and all three felt like friends from the first. So they agreed to help her through Sunday night.

The first move was to find out why the two couples came down to the waterfront. The couples entered a building around the corner from where Evelyn met Vic and Lin, so that is where the three began.

They found the building to be a ticket office run by a lone woman who eyed them suspiciously when Evelyn questioned her. The woman was Chinese and at first spoke English but then lapsed into Cantonese, Pidgin, and shook her head a lot. It was only after considerable persuasion from both Lin and Evelyn that she told them what they wanted to know.

The reason for the visit surprised them all. Both couples booked passage for Monday morning on the Red Dragon, a steamer on its way to China via Hawaii.

Holy cow was Lin's response when she heard it in Chinese and Vic exclaimed the same when Lin told her.

"What's up about the Red Dragon?" Evelyn asked. Vic and Lin were booked to board the Red Dragon on Monday morning.

Things moved even faster after that. Evelyn talked to inspector Blake, an old friend of her uncle Charlie who knew Evelyn, but he said he could do nothing unless the physician confirmed there was a homicide. So Evelyn bought a ticket to share the room with Vic and Lin on the Red Dragon. She contacted Cora and told her what she planned. Then she grabbed a suitcase of things from home and joined Vic and Lin at their hotel. That all happened Saturday.

Sunday morning Cora and Seth came to the hotel and told Evelyn they booked passage on the Red Dragon to Honolulu. "Aunt Ernie was so dear and always so good to me," said Cora. "Seth thinks we should go along to see what happens. Maybe we can help you in some way."

"Besides, we think we might be married in Hawaii," said Seth. "Isn't that right, dear?"

Afternoon Sunday, Evelyn visited Inspector Blake and was gone until sunset. She also visited the Gage estate and talked to the butler and maid. She didn't elaborate further.

The three ate dinner that night in the restaurant of the hotel and talked of many things and eventually the case came up. "I wish that I knew more about poisons," Evelyn told the others, as she leaned back and sipped hot tea. "In my gut I know it was murder. I just know it, and poison is the only method which fits."

"You're probably right," agreed Vic. "Did she eat anything different from everyone else?"

"No. We only got to the first course, the stew, and the butler served everyone from the same serving dish. I thought maybe poison was painted on her plate or the rim of her glass, or her fork or spoon was dipped in poison, but I slipped them each away. Inspector Blake did me a favor and checked them and there was no poison. Besides, even though they are technically suspects I've basically ruled out the butler and maid and they were the ones with best opportunity to do something to the dinnerware. The food could have been poisoned by anyone. Everyone, including me, wandered into the kitchen at some point while dinner was prepared and you could dump poison in a bowl in one second while the cook looked away, but like I said, we were all served from the same dish so it can't be that simple."

"Wow!" said Lin. "Fork dipped poison, rim of the glass painted with poison! You really are some detective! Who else would think of things like that?"

Evelyn smiled and thanked Lin. "But I'm

running out of ideas. I hope I can come up with something before we get to Honolulu."

The three sipped tea in silence for a few moments. Then Lin spoke, "You know, I've thought about how you described the way Miss Gage died. Most poisons would take a little longer or cause abdominal pain, or she may have puked or defecated right there even."

"Holy cow!" Evelyn almost shouted. "I didn't know that. Are you a doctor?"

Vic and Lin laughed and Lin said, "Hardly!" Vic answered the question. "Lin is a pharmacist."

"No kidding!" said Evelyn with a touch of awe in her voice.

Lin explained. Growing up she worked with her parents who practiced Chinese medicine and owned a small shop. She wanted to learn about the herbs and other Chinese remedies from a Western perspective, too, so attended university to become a pharmacist.

"You're really a pharmacist!" Evelyn exclaimed.

"Yes, " smiled Lin. She was very proud of her degree and profession. "I sometimes help at Mortimer's Drug when Mr. Mortimer wants to take time off or things just get really busy. I still help mom and dad, too."

Evelyn frowned and her shoulders drooped. "So maybe I just have a great imagination. Maybe it wasn't murder if you think it wasn't poison."

"Maybe it was murder," answered Lin. "There is something else."

Evelyn got wide-eyed, set her tea down, scooted her chair up to the table, and said to Lin, "Tell me everything you can, please."

33

"Of course," Lin answered and moved her chair closer to the table. "There is a condition called anaphylaxis. It's a very serious allergic reaction which causes throat and lung tissue to swell to the point the person can't breathe and that could make their voice raspy. It can also cause heart failure. Just a few years ago a Frenchman was given the Nobel prize for his work on anaphylaxis. He was researching immunity and injected toxin in dogs. When he repeated the injections a few weeks later, the dogs all died immediately! Turned out, the toxins didn't give immunity, but induced a very severe allergy."

After a moment of silence, Evelyn asked, "How do you trigger such a reaction? Does it require an injection?

Lin answered, "No. Just touch the allergic substance like poison ivy, or breathe it, but a really common way is to drink or eat it."

"Can clams cause it?"

"Absolutely. Shellfish are a very common cause."

Evelyn leaned back and slapped herself on the forehead. "Geez Louise! Would it take much, would it take an actual shellfish? Would juice do it?"

"Juice would do the trick. Doesn't take much. Squeeze a clam, got enough for sure," Lin replied.

Evelyn explained what she was thinking. On the way to the estate with Cora and Seth, she casually asked if they might expect a course of yummy chowder and sourdough for dinner. Cora told her certainly not. Years earlier Miss Gage suffered a reaction to clams that nearly killed her and she was advised to never eat them again. As a result of that incident, she never again allowed

34

sea food of any kind in the house.

"You have a possible method," said Vic.

"Still no fewer suspects. The servants would certainly know the problem and all the family members would likely know about it also. But yes, it is a step closer. The game is afoot!"

Vic and Lin looked at each other and laughed.

"Not another one! You must read Sherlock Holmes. Vic loves Sherlock and is forever saying *the game is afoot*," Lin told Evelyn.

"Really?" Evelyn smiled at Vic. "Well, Sherlock Holmes may be fictional but the plots are brilliant. Every detective should be required to read them." Evelyn paused, then said, "Now I just need to discover who did it. Or maybe who didn't do it. You know, eliminate the impossible and see what's left. I don't yet have a satisfactory answer to why both the other couples are skipping town and now Cora and Seth decided to go, too. Is everyone involved? Wouldn't only a guilty party want to disappear?"

"That does seem to confuse an explanation, doesn't it?" said Lin.

For a moment no one spoke, then Evelyn snapped her fingers, "Or maybe it begins to make things more clear. A guilty party would certainly want to leave, but someone with just a guilty conscience might want to skip out to avoid embarrassing and compromising questions. If you planned to kill someone and someone else beat you to it, wouldn't you be nervous about police interrogation? If police discovered a weapon or incriminating note, you might get pegged for the murder even if you didn't do it! Excuse me for a minute, I need to make some phone calls," Evelyn was obviously excited as she rose and headed for the lobby.

Chapter 3

Mayhem at Sea

All the players were at the dock at sunrise Monday morning, ready to board along with three dozen other passengers, including a Danish priest and his wife headed for Urga.

All the suspects were smiling and cordial, but an undercurrent of tension was evident. Except for Cora and Seth, they were surprised to see Evelyn. They knew by now she was a detective, but Evelyn asked Cora and Seth not to mention she still was on the case. She was just traveling to visit her Uncle and his family in Honolulu in the company of her friends Vic and Lin. Evelyn judged that if her other suspects sensed they were in the clear, they might be more candid in conversation. That first day, she avoided them all until dinner.

The Red Dragon was not strictly a passenger ship. Originally, it served as a cargo vessel, but the passenger trade became so lucrative that it was refitted to accommodate up to 125 passengers, while it also still carried about two thirds the cargo load as before.

The dining tables seated eight persons each. With her six suspects, Evelyn made a table of seven. Vic and Lin sat at another table for all meals. They discussed whether one of them should sit with Evelyn for moral support but decided she didn't need it. Their twenty-five years of life experience offered very little advantage over a lifetime desire to become a detective. She was alone on the case before they met her and she might feel insulted if offered moral support. If she got in trouble or wanted help, fine, but otherwise it was her show.

They would only be aboard ship four nights before they docked in Honolulu. After that first night at dinner, Evelyn paced the cabin and talked to herself as much as to Vic and Lin. She was more sure than ever that four of the suspects disliked Miss Gage substantially, but that didn't help her case.

The next day they were all tourists on a cruise, except maybe Evelyn. She paced the deck, looked deep in thought and seemed eager for dinner.

During dinner, Vic and Lin were highly attentive in an attempt to overhear if Evelyn brought up the case. Early on they heard her do some fishing. She related a famous case which her uncle solved and when finished, she asked "Did you know that if a person has a dangerous medical condition and someone deliberately induces that condition, it is considered murder?"

Later Evelyn casually asked her table mates

how long they would be in Hawaii and two couples were unsure and hadn't arranged return passage. Cora and Seth happily said they would be there long enough to be married and enjoy a proper honeymoon. After that, the conversation centered on wedding ceremonies and great places for a honeymoon.

Following dinner when they all stood to leave, Evelyn positioned herself so she could observe the entire group and offhandedly said she read the medical records of Miss Gage, and discovered she was severely allergic to shellfish. Cora remembered telling Evelyn about the allergy on the drive to dinner and fought a smile, but winked at Evelyn.

Evelyn innocently exclaimed what a sad affliction for a resident of San Francisco and asked if her table-mates knew of the allergy or was it kept a secret. Everyone nodded and said yes they all knew. Evelyn said goodnight and turned to join Vic and Lin, but as the others moved to leave, she did a quick about face and said, "Oh, in Miss Gage's record her doctor said her allergy was so severe that she could die from something called anaphylaxis. I'm curious. The doctor wasn't there to ask and I haven't had a chance at a medical reference. Do any of you know what anaphylaxis is?"

They shook their heads and murmured as they glanced curiously at one another. "I'm afraid no one knows, Miss Chan," said one of the husbands. "That's OK," said Evelyn. "Just curious. I can ask Uncle Charlie when we get to Honolulu. Goodnight." Evelyn turned away and smiled as she approached Vic and Lin. The answers about anaphylaxis were fruitless, but the question caused a posture change for one member of the party. The head and shoulders went back almost imperceptibly, and only a trained eye would catch the change in the jaw line as the muscles tightened. To Evelyn, it was a silent proclamation of mental discomfort.

As soon as they were alone on deck, Vic and Lin questioned Evelyn. "That is a eureka smile if I ever saw one," Lin told her. "Did you get a clue?"

"Nothing for a court but it was sure a clue. Not one I'm happy with, but when murder is done, justice must follow where the clues lead."

When asked what it was, Evelyn said she didn't want to say yet. "When you tell what you know before you know surely, it's just chin music, and gossip from a police officer can cause great harm. I sound more and more like my uncle but it's true." Evelyn suddenly stopped, snapped her fingers and told her friends to go on. She needed to see the captain so turned back toward the dining hall where the captain was still eating.

Vic and Lin decided to walk the deck for a time as it was a lovely night. A host of stars sparkled brightly across the perfectly clear sky, and the damp salt air was comfortably heavy. For a time they watched the lights from a distant ship pass, no doubt headed for San Francisco.

The three left the dining hall which was forward and starboard and strolled casually the long way back to their cabin which was port and aft. When Evelyn left her friends she went through a passageway amidships because it was quicker. There was an intersection with a perpendicular

40

passageway at midpoint and because Evelyn was hurried and deep in thought, she didn't notice a masked figure step out behind her as she passed that juncture. She did, however, feel the solid thump against the back of her head which knocked her to her knees.

Evelyn began to rise, but a burlap bag was pulled down over her head and arms and she was lifted. She twisted and kicked to break free, which made it difficult for the assailant, but he held on. Then Evelyn heard the door opened and the sound of the ship cutting through the water and realized her attacker's intention. He was going to throw her overboard!

She was suddenly icy with fear but not frozen. With the terror came an adrenalin induced surge of strength. Immediately Evelyn began to scream and fight harder. She kicked relentlessly into her captor's shins, but although he growled in pain at each blow, he didn't let go and with the sound of the sea against the ship and the wind, her cries drifted away in the night.

Evelyn felt her captor lean back and raise her higher and she knew he was about to heave her over the rail! She stopped kicking and held her feet together and in a make-this-work-or-die move, Evelyn waited a second until she felt another slightly backward bend of her assailant. Then she drove her feet out in front of her and they caught the rail!

Evelyn pushed with all her might and it worked. The captor was forced back against the bulkhead and the jolt combined with Evelyn's dead weight was too much. She hit the deck hard and instantly rolled away and pulled at the burlap bag as she screamed at the top of her lungs. It only took two seconds to get out of the bag but the deck was deserted. Evelyn jumped up and looked into the walkway but no one was there. She pondered the incident for a moment then continued, more cautiously than before, to see the captain.

Vic and Lin just started to worry when Evelyn finally returned. She told them about the attack, but assured them she was OK. They were curious of course about her mission with the captain, but she was yet mum and said she needed to gather more evidence.

"Sorry, but Uncle Charlie would really frown if I shared suppositions without evidence."

There was a moment of silence, then Vic said, "I need to talk to you about that. Please don't take this wrong. You are not your uncle, Evelyn. You can never be him. I have experience entrusting my efforts to what someone else might presumably do in a situation. We can learn a lot from those who have come before and done before, but we cannot be and are not meant to be them. We learn and build on what we learn from others so some day someone can learn from us. Don't try to be your uncle. Be Evelyn and be the best you can be. I have no doubt whatsoever that someday the name Evelyn Chan will command as much respect as does Charlie Chan."

Evelyn just stared a moment, then said "Thank you," and gave Vic a hug. "No one has ever told me to be me. It's always *why don't you be more like*, or, *why don't you do what so and so did* or *you can't* or the worst of all, *you're a girl*."

From now on, I'm Evelyn Chan, detective, and I will use what I've learned but I'll get the job done my way. There is something I can share, too, although you likely surmised this already. I am no longer working on a hunch. The attack makes it conspicuously obvious, Miss Gage was murdered and the killer is on board!"

When Evelyn returned, she carried a small box and Vic now asked what it was or was it a secret to do with the case. Lin answered for Evelyn, "It's a mahjong set isn't it?"

It was a set Evelyn borrowed from the captain. "Let's play!" she said.

"No," said Vic. "I'm no good at games. I lose too often."

"C'mon, " said Evelyn.

"She's not kidding, Evelyn. She stinks. She always loses."

"Not always!"

"Yes, always, Vic."

"But we need four people," Vic stalled.

"No, we can play with three. I'll show you," said Evelyn. "Do you know how to play with three people, Lin?"

Lin looked at Evelyn with wide eyes and said, "What? Did you really ask me that? Did Beethoven play piano?"

"I'll be a gracious winner, Vic" said Evelyn.

"You? You are forgetting me," said Lin.

"No, I just know how good I am," answered Evelyn with an exaggerated smile and shrug.

"We cannot let that misconception continue," said Lin and pushed Vic toward the table in the center of the cabin. "Sit down Vic, we're playing mahjong!"

"You two are just going to have a shoot out in Dodge with me in the middle! Don't I get a say in this?" Vic asked.

Evelyn and Lin both said with unequivocal sincerity, "Absolutely not. Sit down."

Then Lin said, with a wicked smile, "You don't even need to learn 3 handed well, Vic, since you will lose anyway."

"What? That's not nice!" But Vic smiled, too.

Evelyn said "You two can joke, but mahjong is serious. I apologize up front for my brutality. I plan to maul both of you. Take no prisoners! Or to put it so you understand, Lin, your vicious gung-fu is like patting a kitty cat on the head compared to my savage tiger mahjong."

Lin gasped with a bit of exaggeration and began to tap the table hard with an index finger, "OK! OK! Get that box open. Get the salt and pepper. When you eat your brag, it will taste better if you season it!"

So the three were up until one-thirty in the morning and played eight hands of mahjong. Evelyn and Lin won an equal number of hands and Vic scored a perfect record of losses and all three had fun and never once thought of murder and murderers.

The next day they napped, talked, read, napped, and napped. Twice Evelyn excused herself for a few minutes, but came back mum.

The third night nothing happened. Evelyn was unable to gather further information at dinner. Afterwards, with the help of Vic and Lin, she tried to lay a trap. She strolled around the promenade and passageways for over an hour seemingly alone, but with Vic and Lin always near.

At ten they decided to call it quits and Evelyn

and Lin went back to the cabin, but Vic stayed on deck alone for awhile. The full moon was just a few days away and her thoughts were about another time and another sea beneath the same moon. When Vic leaned over the rail, she closed her eyes and in an instant she walked hand in hand with Nu along a trail on the side of the Barren Hills and was filled with perfect contentment.

"Vic," came a familiar voice from another time. "Vic," it came again and her hand slipped from Nu's hand and she opened her eyes.

Lin laid a hand on Vic's arm and shook her gently. "Vic. I'm sorry I fell asleep and didn't know you weren't back. You've been out here for over two hours! Are you OK?"

Vic turned to Lin, and Evelyn who stood behind her and they both looked startled for just a second and did a double take.

Vic noticed and asked, "What is it?"

"Your eyes. Just for a second they looked as black as mine," Evelyn said.

"They did, Vic," said Lin. "I swear your eyes looked black."

"A trick of the light no doubt," said Vic.

"Had to be a trick of light," said Evelyn. "People's eyes don't change color like that."

The next day was the last full day at sea before they docked at Honolulu. For a great portion of it, the three were on a lower deck fishing with the cook and other crew who lent them fishing gear. Three times Evelyn left at a run, but looked downcast when she returned. They did manage to catch a few small fish, but nothing they could expect to see at the table.

Before dinner, Evelyn dressed quickly and told

45

Vic and Lin she would see them in the dining hall. "Wish me luck!"

Vic shook her head and said, "No. You don't need luck." Then she touched her forehead and then put her hand over her heart and said, "You have all you need here and here, Evelyn."

"Anyone who can tie me in mahjong can out think any criminal. You'll get the killer," said Lin.

Evelyn pulled her shoulders back and said, "You're right. Thanks girls! See you later."

The dining hall was full and Vic and Lin were eating when Evelyn arrived. They looked up and she gave them a big wink and went to sit at her table.

Evelyn brought two folded papers with her, which she slid under her plate as she exclaimed "I'm starved!" Cora asked what the papers were and Evelyn just said, very pleasantly, that she received two interesting telegrams and they would make great after dinner conversation. Vic and Lin were both greatly intrigued and listened intently as on previous nights, yet not once during the meal did they overhear any mention of the case. Once Vic leaned over and whispered to Lin, "Something is afoot, without a doubt."

When everyone at Evelyn's table finished with their meal and her plate was taken, she lifted the telegrams just before a dessert plate was set down. "Oh! That smells great! Is that apple pie?" The server told her it was indeed apple pie, and Evelyn licked her lips and took a full minute to explain how much she loved apple pie. Then one of the wives asked Evelyn about the telegrams.

"Oh yes!" She shared that one telegram was from Miss Gage's attorney and one from her

46

colleague, Inspector Blake with the San Francisco police department. On hearing that, Lin tapped Vic on the hand and whispered, "Hear that! Colleague, not uncle's friend!"

Evelyn stood and began to pace slowly. She asserted there was no doubt whatsoever that Miss Gage was murdered, that the heart attack was not due to natural circumstances. "Her physician was so surprised. He felt she had at least two months or more if she took it easy and the maid and butler both confirmed that she was extremely careful not to exert or excite herself. She was determined to live to change her will and talk to all of you. It meant a lot to her. I am very angry that she was denied that final wish. Miss Gage was murdered and I WILL send the murderer to prison. Folsom has a length of rope just for you!"

Evelyn began to circle the table slowly. She stood behind each person for a time, then moved on. She conspicuously spoke with volume enough that everyone in the dining hall could hear what she said, and by now she held the undivided attention of one and all.

"Then, there was the social situation. From what I have found four of you didn't especially like Miss Gage." One of the men started to protest but Evelyn stopped him. "Nothing is especially incriminating or strange about disliking or having differences with a relative."

Evelyn continued, "Then there was the planned changes to the will. Someone was obviously about to inherit less and someone more. Her attorney could not tell me the particulars of the will, but he did confide that the estate was extensive. In addition to the property which must be worth a tidy sum, Miss Gage's bank accounts totaled nearly three quarters of a million dollars. Many people have been murdered for a great deal less."

"I must admit I was confused for a while. Why is every heir on this ship? However, as the facts were gathered, it became clear that most of you are here from guilty conscience. Whether you made physical preparations for murder or not, you harbored deep-seated ill-will and malicious intent and preferred to avoid any questioning."

Evelyn was back to her chair and leaned forward and smiled "I am probably boring you, so let me get to the crux of the affair."

"Miss Gage died of heart failure and failed blood pressure due to extreme shock brought on by a terribly severe allergy to shellfish. I have consulted with a professional pharmacist and am assured that the condition known as anaphylaxis can kill an allergic person in exactly the manner which we all witnessed Miss Gage die. I further learned shellfish products are known to be a common inducer of this anaphylaxis, and that it would take but a very small amount. It would be undetectable to the tongue in a bowl of beef stew."

At that Lin tapped Vic's hand again, pointed to herself and whispered "Professional pharmacist!"

Evelyn was on a final assault. She told how the police lab, at her suggestion, examined the food and utensils a second time, to look for signs of shellfish, not poison, and indeed found remnants of clam juice in the serving dish that contained the stew.

Evelyn talked with the attorney about the possibility that someone knew the contents of the will. He assured her that was impossible but he did happen to mention that three weeks earlier his office was burglarized. Locks on several file cabinets were broken but the only thing taken was a few dollars from a cash box. Yet, someone could have easily looked at any will in the files and then taken the money to hide the true purpose of the burglary.

The second telegram confirmed that just two days following the burglary at her attorney's office, both the butler and maid observed Miss Gage in a heated discussion with a man in the garden. They couldn't see his face, but voices were raised and the man vaulted the fence to leave rather than take the gate past them.

The first telegram, from Inspector Blake, provided more evidence. "It was about a gang who tried to murder me in San Francisco, but was foiled by my friends and associates, Vic and Lin." By now the entire dining room was so quiet that the proverbial pin dropped would sound like clashed cymbals. "The visitor Miss Gage met in the garden was a member of that gang, she learned of his connection and was going to expose him if he didn't go away on his own." Evelyn gripped the chair back, rocked back on her heels and looked grimly at the heirs.

"What brought it together for me is something Miss Gage told me the night of her death. She wanted those who would benefit from the change in her will to understand it was not due to some goodness on their part. It was cryptic on its own but makes perfect sense with this other information."

"If I didn't already have enough evidence, two nights ago, right here on the Red Dragon, another attempt was made to murder me!" A united gasp buzzed throughout the dining hall and Evelyn paused a moment for effect. With raised voice, Evelyn snapped, "He failed, but I kicked the stink out of his shins and no doubt left incriminating bruises." A single gasp came from Cora as she pressed the back of a hand to her lips and her eyes began to tear.

"I'm truly sorry, Cora," Evelyn said solemnly and directed a harsh gaze to Seth.

Everyone looked at Seth who frowned at first, but suddenly smirked and stood. He glared at Evelyn and growled"You meddling dame, you won't pinch me for this!" His acerbic and vicious tone and countenance caused many diners to recoil in their seats!

Suddenly Seth bolted and was through the door before anyone could react. Every occupant of the dining hall rushed the door after him. Vic, Lin and Evelyn were first out and behind them, the Captain. Seth, however, was nowhere in sight. "Which way did he go?" Evelyn asked with a bit of frustration in her voice. The captain suggested Seth didn't like the sound of the rope Evelyn mentioned, so took the easy way out and jumped overboard.

Cora was beside Evelyn and spoke up, "Seth didn't jump. He's a physical coward and he doesn't know how to swim."

"Then he must be hiding somewhere on board. When we dock in Honolulu I'll get a small army of policemen to search every nook and cranny. We'll find him," Evelyn vowed.

At the mention of an army of police Vic noticed that the captain stiffened and paled a bit.

Evelyn said, "Nothing to do right now. I want my pie," and she went back into the dining hall.

"Geez, Evelyn, you like to eat as much as Vic!" said Lin.

"I like apple pie," replied Evelyn.

Vic said, "Food is good for you, Lin." Then she invited the captain to join them, and with stern, unblinking eye contact added, "Please."

The other passengers had retired to their cabins. Vic, Lin, Evelyn, Cora and the Captain sat at a table and the cook brought them slices of fresh apple pie. "What is it, Captain?" asked Vic. "You didn't seem too happy at the suggestion of police searching your vessel."

Evelyn looked at Vic, then the Captain, swallowed some pie and asked, "Is there a problem, captain?"

He replied that he simply preferred not to have police on board and that it might keep them in port over schedule. Evelyn assured him that all she wanted was the murderer.

Vic made fists, leaned forward and spoke again. She made no attempt to disguise the menace in her voice. "Do you deal in people, Captain? Is this a slave ship? I despise slavers! They are less than human, and don't deserve their next breath and given the opportunity I would personally take the last breath from every one of them!"

The indignance and shock could not be forged. Vic judged them to be real. "My God, no!" The captain was not a man given to fear but Vic's tone and posture sent a chill down his spine for they were not empty words. He was a man of great and varied experience and could tell that Vic's statement was not an idle threat but spoken on authority of her own experience.

"Do you take opium to my country," asked Vic and watched the captain closely. "No!" The captain snapped and again Vic sensed his sincerity.

"Then I am agreed with Evelyn, our only concern in this matter is that a murderer be brought to justice."

Then Cora spoke, "Seth murdered my dear aunt and attempted to kill Detective Chan and he must pay for his crimes."

For several moments there was silence then the captain crossed his forearms and leaned forward on the table. "I'm not Chinese," he began.

"You're Mongolian," said Lin and Evelyn together and looked at each other with a nod.

"I've seen photos of my parents' Mongolian friends from before they came to the United States. You just look Mongolian to me," said Lin.

"When I was in your cabin to borrow the mahjong I saw your name in the log on your desk," said Evelyn. "I have a Mongol friend with the same name, Chuluun.

The captain nodded and smiled. "This is a time of turmoil in my country. Even in a country where life is naturally rugged, these days it is doubly so. Simple, daily survival can be very difficult for my people...."

Vic held up a hand and said "Stop. If you are helping your people, without harming others, we don't need to know more. We can never reveal something we don't know. Leave it there."

"Couldn't your men search the ship now?" Evelyn asked.

"They could do a better job and faster than the police who don't know the ship," said Lin. "They'll miss some sleep but for a good cause. Or for two good causes."

"They could. They will," nodded the Captain and he rose. Vic, Lin and Evelyn would wait in the dining hall, and the Captain would walk Cora to her cabin then muster the crew to begin the search. Before he could get out the door Evelyn held up her plate and asked, "Captain, would you mind if...." Before Evelyn finished, Captain Chuluun called to the cook to bring out a whole pie, then left with Cora.

About one in the morning Evelyn finished the last of the pie and pushed her plate away. Lin bent over and looked under the table and said, "I don't understand."

"What?" Evelyn asked and she and Vic both looked under the table.

"Where did that big pie go?" Lin asked.

Vic laughed and Evelyn answered simply, "Apple is my favorite."

A few minutes later they heard someone running on the deck and expected Captain Chuluun, but when the door burst open it was Seth with a .45 in his hand and murder in his eye!

Seth didn't pause as he pushed through the door. As he came, he raised the pistol at Evelyn.

Vic's hand was on the plate in front of her and she grasped it the instant she recognized Seth.

Vic saw there could be no talk, no time to stall. She knew that if Seth made it all the way to the table it would be too late. Someone would die.

"You and your bimbo friends..." Seth muttered

53

as he neared the table.

"Next!" Vic rapped even as she drew the plate across her body with her right hand. At the same time she slammed Evelyn on a shoulder with her open hand and knocked her off her chair.

Lin understood their *magic word*, saw what was happening, and grabbed her plate.

Seth's gun fired!

Vic slung the plate toward Seth and it hit his gun arm at the biceps and he dropped his weapon.

No sooner did Seth drop the gun when Lin's plate hit him hard in the forehead, snapped his head back, and he crumpled to the floor.

Vic and Lin were both up and moving immediately. Vic kicked the .45 away from the unconscious Seth. Lin took a lace from one of his shoes, rolled him on his stomach and tied his hands behind him. Seth began to rouse as she finished and Lin slapped the back of his head. "I don't like to be called bimbo! The way you won't like being called fish when you start to flop at the end of that rope."

Evelyn watched them and rubbed her shoulder. "I will definitely have a bruise on this shoulder, but it's better than being shot." She half turned toward her chair and stuck a finger in the bullet hole in the chair back. "Right about where my heart would've been. You guys are good!"

Just then the door burst open and the Captain and two of his men came in. He stopped when he saw Seth on the floor and slipped the revolver he carried back into his belt. "I see you got your man, detective. My men will lock him up and watch him until we dock."

Evelyn went to the radio room and sent a wire to Honolulu police. Vic and Lin woke Cora and told her. Then the three friends met up at their cabin, with the intention to rest a couple of hours, but the evening had been far too dramatic to let them sleep, so they talked.

Evelyn told Vic and Lin the second telegram included information which would please them. She asked Inspector Blake if a body was found down near the bay. She wanted to confirm a reason for the attack and questioned the inspector without admitting she was there. It turned out the man was a member of a group called the Ragland Gang and Inspector Blake found that one of the members was a Seth Malone who went by many alias last names.

The young detective pieced it all together. Originally, Seth wanted her around for cover. After all, a murderer wouldn't want a detective around, and if a detective witnessed Miss Gage apparently die of a heart attack, that would be the end of it. He evidently considered Evelyn incompetent, but became concerned when he saw she was suspicious and followed the other heirs. So he sent the gang to get rid of her. That didn't work, thanks to Vic and Lin. When Seth learned Evelyn was joining the cruise, he worried she might rule out the others which would narrow the field a bit too much, so he needed to stop her.

As far as the incident near the docks, Inspector Blake told Evelyn that a waitress at an Italian restaurant saw three girls "beat the tar" out of five men and one of the men got killed when he pulled a gun. Evelyn asked if, theoretically, someone

55

was about to be killed and someone else came to help and things happened like the waitress said, would the people in the theoretical situation be in much trouble. In a rather indirect manner, the inspector told Evelyn that particular death was designated as gang related and the theoretical people acted in self-defense and there would be a lot, emphasis on a lot, of theoretical paper work if the incident needed to be rewritten to include others who might be theoretically involved.

"Which I think means," Evelyn told them, "that none of us should worry about going to jail," which was a relief to both Vic and Lin.

"I'm glad Seth is caught but I wish I could have prevented murder in the first place as intended."

"You did," Vic said. "There is no doubt that Miss Gage would have died anyway, and very shortly after their wedding, Cora would have been victim to an unfortunate accident. You prevented Cora's murder and Miss Gage would be pleased. She planned to disinherit Cora so Seth would have no reason to marry her and kill her later. Now Cora will get her inheritance and Seth will get his proper reward, too!"

Within minutes of docking, the Red Dragon was boarded by five policemen. The ranking man was Inspector Hu and he knew Evelyn. Young Detective Chan took full charge and told Inspector Hu she would come to the station and write a full report later. Vic and Lin were proud of the confident, self-assured professional their new friend metamorphosed into.

The Red Dragon had a one night stay only. Vic,

Lin and Cora stayed over at the Chan residence and they had a swell time. Cora was invited to stay and see the island with Evelyn while she was there, and those two drove Vic and Lin down to the Red Dragon the next morning. When Vic and Lin boarded, the Captain welcomed them and thanked them for how they handled the situation with Seth. Soon, the Red Dragon began to ease away and Vic and Lin leaned over the rail to wave 'bye to Evelyn and Cora on the dock.

VIC: MONGOL

Chapter 4

Beyond the Great Wall !

Four days after the Red Dragon left Honolulu it made a 24 hour stop in Yokohama, Japan. Vic and Lin went ashore and tried some curry rice, fish (raw, steamed and battered), fried tako, buckwheat noodles in broth with green onions and udon, miso soup, pickled vegetables, grilled unagi, yakitori, and plenty of other goodies. To finish off the excursion they purchased a bag of red bean paste anpan to take with them.

Two days later there was a 24 hour stop in Kirun, Formosa which the captain called Kelang, the old name before Formosa came under Japanese control. Then the Red Dragon doubled back North into the East China Sea and docked at Dairen where Vic and Lin entered China.

The pier was busy, but not with tourists. It was mostly dock workers unloading ships. Friends came for the missionaries and after they were gone, Vic and Lin were the only passengers who remained from the Red Dragon. Impatient, they were already questioning how long they should wait when a young man about their age approached and spoke to Lin in Chinese. The man and Lin shook hands, and bowed, then laughed and launched into a conversation. After a couple of minutes, Lin said, "Excuse my impoliteness. This is my friend Vic. Vic, this is cousin Lao."

Vic shook hands with Lao and bowed from the shoulders as Lin taught her. "Ni hao," she said.

"Ni hao," Lao answered. "I am pleased to meet you Vic Challenger! I have read the story of you and the jaguar. I was most impressed," he told her.

Vic blushed a bit and said, "Thank you, Lao. I am honored. I am relieved also that you speak such fluent English. I have exhausted my knowledge of Chinese."

"It is not for you to worry," Lao told her. "I will be entirely at the service of you and my cousin while you are in China, and I have arranged for a very good friend named Chu to guide you in Mongolia. You are in good hands with my cousin, also. Although she has been raised in an English speaking country, her Chinese is flawless." At this Lin thanked Lao in English and then the two reverted to Chinese and began walking. Vic followed and took mental notes to write about later and just enjoyed the new sights.

They only walked one block when the smell of food triggered the usual response. "Mm mm! That smells good!" Vic said and walked over to a street vendor cooking meat on a portable grill. "Oh, those look like squirrel legs. I love squirrel," Vic said. Lao laughed. Lin said, "I don't know for sure but from what my parents told me that isn't squirrel, Vic."

Vic looked at it a moment, then said. "Oh. They're a big rat's hind legs, huh?"

Lao nodded.

"Well," said Vic, "We can call it street squirrel. It looks good and smells really good. I think I'll have some. Do either of you want some?" Lao told her he wasn't hungry and Lin said, with just a little hesitation, "OK. I told my parents I would eat and do as many things as I could to experience their homeland. I guess rat drumsticks would be a good place to begin."

"These may not be fresh," said Lao. "Sometimes, meat on the street may be what didn't sell on the day before. Let's go to a restaurant where you can get a whole, fresh rat." Lao was from Peking but knew Dairen and in a few minutes they stopped at an outdoor restaurant. An overhead plank door was propped open in the side of a building. There was a counter and behind it was a grill with pots boiling something, a worktable and one man and two women.

In front of the restaurant there was a long narrow table with bench seats. Two bamboo cages were stacked at one end of the counter and each held about a dozen live rats. "Here we can get fresh meat," said Lao. He greeted the man behind the counter then turned to Vic and Lin. "Pick the one you want."

"Pick one? How?" Lin asked. "What's the difference? They all just look like rats."

"If you are really hungry you pick a large one, otherwise a small one. Look for good coat. If its hair is falling out it may be sick and taste bad. If he is lively the meat will be more lean. A large rat that doesn't move much will have more fat."

Lin seemed a bit hesitant so Vic said, "I've eaten armadillo, opossum and squirrel. They are all rodents and good. And you ate squirrel at my house before and liked it."

The two chose their rats and the man behind the counter reached into a cage. "I know. I'm sure I'll like it," said Lin. Then she began, "How do they k..." Her question was answered before she got it out. The man pulled a rat from the cage by its tail, flipped his wrist and sent the rat into a high arc. It fell behind the counter head first and made a soft thud when its head hit the brick floor. The man bent over and grabbed the rat and tossed it onto the table in front of a woman who immediately began to gut and skin it. Vic chose a plump rat and in seconds the other woman had it on the prep table. In just a few minutes, two well done rats were set in front of them and Lin admitted, "It does smell pretty good." They ate tentatively at first, but in the end only picked skeletons and rat heads remained.

Shortly, they were at the train station to begin an hour wait for the train to Peking. They were surprised when the Danish missionaries and their friends arrived and boarded the same train. Lao and Lin shared a seat and spoke in Chinese most of the trip. Vic chatted with the missionaries and their friends to learn about Mongolia directly from Westerners who lived there.

"We don't have permits to enter Mongolia, and our ship Captain said it may be difficult. Do you have any suggestions?" Vic asked the missionaries from Urga. They told her don't draw attention to yourself, act like you know what you're doing even if you don't, and don't even apply for permits. "You won't like this, but they don't pay much attention to women."

Lao heard this and nodded his agreement. "I have a friend who is a head guard at the wall in Kalgan where you will enter Inner Mongolia and from there it is no problem. They are correct, it is likely you could not get permits. On the other hand, the government will not care if you go without them. They do not like to give permits to foreigners because you might get killed and your country would blame them. However, if you go without a permit, it doesn't matter. The blame will not be theirs but yours."

"Holy cow, Lao," said Lin, "is it really that dangerous?"

"It could be. Depends on where you go and how lucky you are."

"Oh. I like that. We won't get killed if we are lucky," said Lin, sarcastically.

Vic said, "Mexico was having a revolution and I saw nothing of it. Lao is probably right that it depends on where we go."

"Yes, but I think beyond the Great Wall will yet be more dangerous than Mexico. They were near a conclusion to their revolution. The same is not true in Mongolia. There are too many hands in the pot. The Chinese took control of Mongolia last year. The Russians want to push them out. Mongols want their own country. There are rogue Russians who would have

Mongolia for themselves. There are Mongol bandits, often led by rogue Russians, and Chinese bandits, the Red Beards, who kill anyone they like and take whatever they want. They are the biggest danger. Both Russia and China want to seem friendly to the Mongol people to gain favor. The rogues don't care about favor. Chu told me there are rumors that a renegade Russian, Baron von Ungren has raised an invasion force. He plans to rule as the new Genghis Khan, and he condones and encourages his forces to every known atrocity. Chu will know how best to avoid danger. If you want to see rugged country and wild animals Vic, Chu can do a very good job for you, and hopefully avoid the conflict."

"Who is Chu?" Lin asked. "Sounds Chinese."

"He is," said Lao. "But he married a Mongol woman and has lived there about six years now. He used to lead trading caravans with his father into the most remote places, on the old trails where the trains don't go. That is how he met his wife. We grew up together. His parents still live in the house next to my family."

"Sounds like a perfect guide," Vic said.

"He is. Besides Chinese and Mongolian, he also speaks English and Russian well and he has friends throughout Mongolia from his days on the caravans. At the gate you will meet Chin, another friend. The three of us were always together when we were kids."

They reached Peking an hour before sunset, and after farewells to the missionaries, hired rickshaws for a one hour ride to Lao's home. When they arrived, the household immediately became a hive of activity. They were served tea and cakes and Lin answered questions for two hours. Lin's aunt Jing-Wei, Lao's mother and the sister of Lin's mother, spoke a bit in English, as when she welcomed Vic, but mostly they spoke Chinese. At one point the aunt laughed and clapped her hands and Vic asked what that was about.

"She told me she was so glad her sister raised a big family and she gets to meet her eldest," Lin couldn't stop smiling. "She is really neat and she misses my mom. Mom is her little sister. They haven't seen each other for almost thirty years! They were really close as little girls, though, and have written each other twice every year, without fail. Every Lunar New Year and every autumn. My mom keeps every letter and I've seen them. They almost fill a hat box!"

The next evening there was a dinner attended by what seemed to be every distant relative of Lin. The family was fairly well to do and several large tables were set up outside within a fenced area and Vic counted 63 adults seated. Many children who ranged in ages from what looked like maybe four up to ten or so played near the tables.

As is the way at dinner in a Chinese household, whenever Vic's plate seemed to have an empty area, someone would rush to fill it. At one point Lin came over to tell Vic a secret. "I know you love to eat, Vic, but your plate may never empty no matter how much you eat. And you might actually find something you don't like that much."

"Why are you whispering," Vic whispered.

"I'm not sure. It may be rude to tell you this

with the host and hostess here, but mom told me that everyone does this. When you are full, leave just a bite of each food on the plate. If you don't like something or there is too much, call one of the children over and give it to her, or him, and smile. You will be seen as generous and compassionate. If you take a bite first and smile as though you enjoy it, then give the rest to a child, you will be seen as even more generous and compassionate. The children learn fast and will begin to gather near you in hopes you will feel generous again. They like everything so will take anything you don't like – if there is such a thing!"

Two days later, they were up and on the move early. They left their dresses and Mary Janes with Lin's aunt and caught a train to Kalgan. Even though the Great Wall at that point was in disrepair, Vic and Lin were thoroughly impressed. Armed soldiers were at the gate and eyed everyone. They waved some travelers through without a second glance, while others were stopped and questioned and a few were searched.

All the soldiers but one were armed with rifles. It was the one with a .45 that Lao went to. "Chin!" called Lao and the man turned to him. They bowed and talked good-naturedly for several minutes. Then Lao introduced Lin and Vic and told his friend Chin they were visiting Mongolia to take photographs and maybe go wolf hunting.

Beyond the gate the area seemed no different for a distance, then the crude structures became fewer and fewer. Finally, when buildings were about to run out, they came to a low block structure with a large open barn surrounded by pens which housed a large number of horses and camels. Several automobiles were parked inside the barn, all open coupes in dire need of paint. Seated on the back of one was a man of about thirty who jumped up when he saw them. It was Chu.

After Vic and Lin were introduced, Lao and Chu talked for almost an hour. "I hope you both can ride a horse well. If not, you will learn," Chu laughed. "Lao thinks you can ride."

They assured Chu they could ride, but perhaps not as well as a Mongol, since they are renowned for horsemanship. On the steppes and in the deserts, distances can be great between habitations or water, and a horse can be the difference between life and death. Just as horse theft earned you a hanging in the Old West of America, a horse thief in Mongolia would be killed immediately when found by the owner.

"But," said Chu when he saw Vic and Lin eyeballing the corral, "we won't go horseback from here. We don't have the time to go the distances. This is our ride for now," and he patted the boot of a large heavy convertible.

Vic's first question was, "Do we need to change our dollars into Mongolian money? Will it make things easier?"

Chu answered, "Mongolia does not have its own currency. You probably won't need money but if you do, you can use your dollars or British pounds or Russian rubles or Yanchan, the Chinese Mexican dollar. You can also use salt or tsai bricks, tea bricks in English. Trading posts as this one will always take most any of those."

Chu suggested Vic obtain some rubles, some

67

salt and tsai and keep some dollars.

"How do you want to be paid?" Vic asked.

Chu got a strange look and said, "You don't pay me. You are Lao's friends."

"Yes I pay you. My boss provided money for a guide and Lao said you are a guide. We will be here two months or more. You can't guide us around for free. You must earn a living." Lin and Lao also assured Chu it wasn't wrong to charge them. "It's two things. We will be friends and our tour will be business," Lin finally convinced Chu.

Once Chu agreed they went into the trading post and came out with some rubles, bags of salt blocks and tsai bricks, extra batteries for their electric lights, and American military surplus canteens. After short goodbyes to Lao, Vic and Lin threw their packs into the back seat and Vic jumped in with them. Lin rode up front with Chu. Vic took the watch out of her pocket and noted, "Three p.m. I'm not likely to need this for awhile," and she stowed the watch in the bottom of her pack.

As they rode, Chu told them about his days with caravans and about how he met his wife. It was obvious he missed her and he admitted as much, and also said he worried because there was so much lawlessness in Mongolia at the time. "At times there can be even more trouble for my family. Most Mongols think a Mongol woman should never marry a Chinese and many Chinese think no worthy Chinese should wed a Mongol. Then the twins! My daughters are orles, half breeds, and looked down on by both races." Chu drove in silence for a minute then said, "My baby girls are the most beautiful in the world. Just wait. You'll see!"

Then Chu explained about dangers, warning them first that if they see a group of men, avoid them. It didn't matter who they were. "If they don't like you or don't trust you, or if you have something they want, you will be in danger."

"Ugh! I've heard that advice before, in Mexico. Why is it that so often, whenever people get in a group, they want to hurt and kill other people? It disgusts me." Chu didn't understand the word disgust so Vic explained and Lin told him in Chinese.

"It is disgusting, isn't it!" agreed Chu.

The greater dangers, Chu told them, were the rogue Russians and the Hung-hu-tzes, or Chinese Red Beards. "White Russians are those who supported the tsar in the 1917 Revolution. They are not faring well in the ongoing civil war. The Hung-hu-tzes are bandits that have existed for centuries. Both are dangerous and kill anyone they wish and take whatever they want."

"Most feared by everyone is the Mad Baron. He is a White Russian with great experience at war, but said by some to be insane. He has amassed a large force to invade Mongolia, but I hear that his recruitment efforts have slowed."

"If less men join him that's good," said Lin.

"Yes, but the reason is what Vic would call disgusting. He held a large recruitment day and, because of his reputation, thousands came to join him. He inspected every man personally and if a man possessed any physical defect or any Jewish blood, the Baron killed him on the spot. So now, one who doubts his perfection is hesitant to enlist with the Baron. Most battles occur farther

North, especially around Urga, but it can spread anywhere, so we must stay wary and hope the Mad Baron stays in Russia."

By then they were away from Kalgan. "Did Lao give you weapons? He told me you can both shoot," said Chu as he stopped the auto. Vic and Lin both raised their shirt a couple of inches to reveal Colt .45 double action revolvers Lao loaned them. "He gave us fifty rounds each," Vic said. Chu got out and walked back to the boot. He pulled out a wool blanket and unwrapped three semi-auto carbines. "Winchester carbines, 20-inch barrel so they're easy to use on a horse, .351 caliber and the magazine holds 20 rounds. We each have three magazines."

Chu gave Vic and Lin each a carbine and a box of cartridges. "These are fine weapons," said Vic. "Looks like French writing on the stock. How did you get your hands on these?"

Chu told them about eighteen months earlier three men appeared one day from nowhere and hired him as a guide. They spoke English and Russian and just made maps and didn't want Russians or Chinese to know. A very quiet and mannered giant man was in charge. The others called him O. "When they left, I took them to the steppes where an aeroplane landed for them. I asked O earlier if I could just have a rifle and some ammunition for my pay instead of money since they would be more useful, and I might need them to protect my family. Before they climbed aboard the plane, O told his two men to throw their weapons on the ground along with his and all their ammunition, and then he pulled 2 full cases of ammunition from the plane and dropped them. Before he climbed in he said, *Chu, I've lost my weapons somewhere, doggonit. It means a godawful lot of paperwork, but if they ever show up it'll mean even more paperwork and I don't like paperwork. Thank you for your help and take care of your family.*"

Vic thought O sounded very familiar. "Were they French?" Vic asked.

"No. I'm sure they were American."

"Did this O have arms bigger than your legs, stand about two meters and have a soft voice?" Chu said yes.

"Did you hear the names of the other men?" Vic asked.

"They also only used letters. One was GQ and the other was JJ," answered Chu.

Vic half smiled and shook her head,"Oh, my... Did the one called JJ wear six guns like a cowboy?"

Chu said, "Yes! And a big cowboy hat and he had sand colored hair and always looked ready to jump. Do you know these men Vic?"

Lin looked back at Vic and said, "Yeah, Vic, do you know them? They sound kind of cloak and dagger or maybe Uncle Sammish. How would you know them?"

"I'm pretty sure I've met them. Oliver, I never learned his last name, and Jimmie Jones. I don't know about GQ. I met the others briefly in Mexico. My but they do get around."

"How did you meet them? I never heard them in the story of your Yucatan trip. What did you leave out?" asked Lin.

Vic didn't answer and by now Chu had the

71

auto rolling again. They were on a trail turned road, used by wagons and horses and camels for centuries, and they followed it for several miles through a deep gorge. Chu told them that for centuries the gorge was a common route used by Mongols to invade China. Chu probably never got the automobile over about 25 miles per hour on the better parts, but it was a guess because the speedometer didn't work. Vic noticed Lin looked a bit sullen so leaned up and whispered, "I'm sorry Lin. It's just something no one needed to hear, but now that we are working together I will tell you later and...tell about something else that began in Africa. OK?" Lin nodded.

While in the gorge, they stopped a few times for Vic to snap photos. Then later when they climbed to the Mongolian plateau and were on the steppes, they stopped for Vic to take a photo of *nothingness.* "And I thought the grasslands of Nebraska could look desolate," said Vic. Lin added, "Grass and wheat look like a forest compared to this."

"Much of Mongolia is beautiful," said Chu. "There are mountains and forests and lakes and rivers. Though Westerners think of desert with the name Gobi, much of it is what you call prairie.

"I know, Chu," Vic said. "Personally, I think this is beautiful. Wide open, uncluttered, free, unlike anything many of my readers have ever experienced." They were all silent for several minutes, then Vic said, "Hear that?"

Lin asked, "What? All I hear is my own heartbeat."

Vic nodded, "Exactly. Isn't it wonderful?"

Chu told them, "If you are unfortunate enough

to be in a sand storm you may hear the opposite of silence, the banshees of hell as they wander the sands in search of souls. I don't think you will like that sound."

Just before dark, Chu drove off the road for a distance he called one li, and parked behind a small thicket of scraggly trees. Vic told Lin a li was half a kilometer or about one third mile. Lin smiled and replied, "It is also the name of a very prominent family in Nebraska."

The temperature was in the mid-fifties in the daytime but as the sun disappeared, it dropped quickly so they all pulled jackets out of their packs. They built a small fire on the opposite side of the car from the road and Chu brought out a can of corned beef and a can of hardtack for each of them. They were from the trading post in Kalgan. "These are American military rations. Rations are given to soldiers in packages, but merchants tear them apart and sell the separate items to make more profit," Chu told them.

"Ok," said Chu as they ate, "Lao told me you two want to take photos and do some hunting. Is there anything you especially want to see or shoot?"

Vic and Lin told him they each wanted to bag a wapiti and wolf. Vic wanted photos of scenery, animals and plants and Mongols in native dress, a ger, and generally anything uncommon or exotic to most of her readers.

Chu didn't understand wapiti but when they described it, he said, "Oh, you want to shoot a maral. Easy enough! First stop is Dalan bulag, 70 Springs. It is what you might call a frontier town. It is the first place we come to and it will take all day tomorrow and a little more the next day to arrive."

Chu was silent a moment as he reached into one of their "money" bags to pull out a dark brown block, tsai leaves pressed together to make a brick. "Would you both like tsai?" They both answered yes so Chu set out three tin cups beside the fire. Then he scraped the tsai brick with a knife and let the shavings fall into the cups. "It's that easy and you cannot drink money in your country." He poured hot water over the shavings and handed Vic and Lin each a cup.

"From Dalan bulag we go to the mountains and my family. There we take horses and make runs for maral and wolf if we don't see one before we get there. Then we will cross some dunes for photos and I will show you a canyon where there is art from very long ago."

"Like cave art? Like ancient men would have made?" Vic asked. "I would really like to see that."

Chapter 5

Dalan Bulag

Hardtack and coffee served as the sunrise breakfast for Vic and Lin. "Have a cup of George?" Vic asked Chu. It was instant coffee actually named Red E Coffee but was the product child of George C. L. Washington, and soldiers during the Great War nicknamed it *cup of George.* Chu stuck with his tsai.

That day was mostly driving. They stopped a few times for photos and once for lunch. For the most part, the scenery didn't change, dirt and brown grass out of sight, and even to someone seeing it for the first time, it soon became monotonous. The road changed now and then, from bad to worse, and forced Chu to slow to a crawl because of potholes or large rocks in the road.

Two hours into the drive that day, Lin asked, "When will the scenery change?"

Chu laughed and said, "Not this day. Didn't you look at a map before coming here?"

"Of course," said Lin, "we looked at lots of maps, but a flat paper on a table doesn't really look the same, no matter how you try to imagine."

"We have numbers in our head," said Vic, "but until you are here, and look ahead and behind, and see nothing to the horizon, it is difficult to imagine the distances."

"Well now you are down on that map. Let me try to describe where you are on the paper and where we will go," said Chu.

"Kalgan is where we met at the Great Wall, or Lao may have called it Dongkou, the Eastern gate, and it is a Chinese city. We have been traveling northwest. The distance from Kalgan to Dalan bulag is about 200 kilometers.

"That's about 125 miles," said Vic to Lin.

Chu glanced back and said, "That was fast."

"She's a numbers nut," said Lin. "Mathematician."

"Numbers are interesting, not to mention useful," defended Vic. "How else could you warn your…. friends how many bandits are coming or how many maral are in the herd?"

Chu nodded and continued. "From Kalgan, we traveled across Inner Mongolia which is an autonomous region of China. Now we are in Mongolia, a separate nation. From Dalan bulag, we continue northwest. We will avoid crossing the els or empty sands. We could visit beautiful canyons to the west of Dalan bulag, but I think you will find it more interesting to explore other canyons that have been seen by fewer people, even Mongols. We will travel another two and a half days beyond Dalan bulag to reach my home. There we will park this automobile, and use horses to hunt wolf and maral. Then we will ride across the els, where they are narrow, to the canyon with the ancient art."

When Chu pulled off the road as the night before, the sun was just down. Although its light was no longer on the ground, it made the western sky white yellow which turned to blue then black. Dinner was a repeat of the night before. As they sipped coffee and tsai, Chu told more stories of the days leading caravans with his father, and Vic followed with stories of big game hunting in Africa.

As they crawled into their pup tents, Lin told Vic, "Thanks for inviting me to come with you, Vic. You and Chu have such neat adventures to tell. The best adventure I can talk about is our trip to Chicago."

"Oh, Lin! Thank you for coming! I am so glad you are here. I would have asked you to go to Mexico, but the only trips we ever made together were to Lincoln and Chicago, so for some stupid reason I just assumed you would prefer more civilized travel. I won't make that mistake again. I'm sure we will have a little adventure here. Wolf hunting ought to be exciting. And adventure is measured by experience of the adventuress. At the time, shopping in Chicago was a fantastic adventure to both of us!"

Most of the next day and evening were the same. The one difference happened in the afternoon when they scared up a flock of prairie chickens and managed to shoot two for dinner.

On the third day, early light heralded the coming sunrise when they were up and the sun itself just topped the horizon when they pulled away. They sighted Dalan bulag one hour out of camp and reached it an hour later.

There wasn't much to Dalan bulag. A dozen stone buildings and 5 times that number of gers. Chu knew where to go and stopped at a single level block structure. Men loitered outside and horses and camels milled around in small corrals beside the building. Just before they came to a stop, Chu said, "Put your revolvers where they can be seen, nod but do not smile if you pass someone. Some of the men may be bandits, and many have never imagined, let alone seen, a woman from the west nor eyes like yours, Vic. Try to look mean or, as they would say in Mexico, like a bad hombre."

Vic and Lin looked at each other. "I'll see what I can do," said Vic. Lin said to Chu, "So I already look like a bad hombre?"

Chu held his laugh and answered, "Chinese women are not as rare here."

Vic and Lin carried their revolvers inside their pants with their flannel shirts draped over them, so before they climbed out of the auto, they tucked in their shirts, to place the revolvers in plain view.

As they walked toward the entrance, a group of five men eyed them and just before they reached the door, one stepped in front of Chu and nodded toward Vic and Lin and spoke in Mongolian in an obviously unfriendly tone. He looked at the other men, spoke quietly, then laughed unpleasantly. Then he abruptly stopped smiling and laid his hand on the holstered pistol which hung from his neck by a leather cord.

Chu kept his eye on the men and said to Vic and Lin, "He doesn't think a Chinese should have a gun, especially a woman, and he thinks you are Russian Vic, and he likes Russians even less; but whatever you are you shouldn't have a gun."

"Whatever…." Vic started and looked straight at the man, with the most offensive 'bad hombre' look she could muster. "Would it help if he knew we can find the trigger?"

Chu said, "Huh? What do...."

Before he could spit his question out, Vic said to Lin, "There are a lot of rocks around here. Let's do our rock routine." Lin nodded and they both bent down. Both kept their eyes on the men and each took up a rock roughly the size of a softball. "Next!" said Vic and underhanded her rock straight up. Lin drew and fired and hit it twice before it dropped to head level.

Immediately Lin underhanded her rock. Vic drew and fired. Her target wasn't as solid and the first slug cracked it in two, so Vic fired twice more and hit both halves before they were down to head level. The whole episode didn't take more than six seconds. Vic turned and held her revolver at her hip, pointed toward the man who did the talking.

Suddenly a man burst from the building. He spewed Mongolian loud and fast and waved a long shotgun! When he saw Chu, he smiled and lowered the gun, but kept talking loud and fast. Chu nodded toward the men and said something and the man from the building looked toward them and they turned and walked away. Vic watched them and noticed that Lin also kept her revolver out and pointed meaningfully. "Lin, it's scary how much we sometimes think alike." They holstered their revolvers but kept them in sight.

Chu introduced the man as Bat and they followed him inside. Bat only spoke Mongolian so Chu explained that Bat was a good friend of his father's for many years. This business was half his and half his sisters'. It was the local store, surplus, garage, stable, restaurant and bar. Bat took them to a table and got them seated and called to someone. He sat with them and talked with Chu, loud and fast and patted Chu on the shoulder every few words.

After a few minutes a woman came out with several dishes. She placed a bowl in front of each of them including one for herself and centered a tray on the table. Then she went around and hugged Chu. The woman was fifty or better and her skin was toughened and dark from the harsh weather and sun on the steppes. Nonetheless, Vic and Lin were still taken by her good looks, her perfect oval face framed by thick, still black hair, high cheek bones, a radiant smile and almond eyes which sparkled like those of a ten year old.

Chu introduced her, "This is Bayarmaa, my...my lawless mother I think."

Vic and Lin looked at each other puzzled, then Lin asked Chu, "Do you mean mother-in-law? The mother of your wife?"

"Yes!" said Chu. "My wife's mother! And Bat is her brother."

While conversation continued among Chu and Bayarmaa and Bat, Vic and Lin ate.

The bowls in front of them held a thick stew of hearty chunks of meat, most still attached to bone, with carrots and cabbage and it gave off a delicious smell. "Khorkhog," Chu told them. "It can be prepared with any meat but this is goat." From the platter they took dumplings which Chu called khuushuur, meat filled and deep fried in sheep fat. "Bat says the meat is zeer he shot yesterday," Chu told them. After Chu described it, Vic and Lin realized that a zeer was a local antelope.

Vic and Lin both ate all the stew, and two

dumplings then suddenly found their bowls filled again by an old man who appeared quietly from the kitchen. Then he reached into the large pocket of his apron and pulled out two more dumplings and placed them in front of Vic and Lin.

"If you get your fill, leave a little. Otherwise he will continue to bring more," Chu told them.

However, that didn't seem like an imminent problem. Both thoroughly enjoyed the food, although Vic was slowed a tad as she made notes in her journal.

Chu enjoyed a very lengthy conversation with his in-laws while Vic and Lin ate a lot. They also roamed around the store and then they went outside. Vic got her camera and took photos of the stables, gers, and buildings, and pretty much the whole settlement in a dozen shots.

Around noon Chu was ready to leave. Bat brought out gas cans and refilled the cans in the boot of the car and then he filled the tank. They hadn't touched the two water cans in the boot, but all needed to refill their canteens. Vic gave Chu about half the rubles and dollars and asked him to pay for the gas and get anything else they needed or which he wanted. Vic and Lin then said goodbye and through Chu's translation profusely thanked his in-laws. Chu came out, after Vic and Lin, with two bags. One was a large burlap bag he carried on a shoulder and dropped in the back floor beside Vic.

Lin reached back and opened the bag to find it full of flat round chunks of what looked like dried grass held together with something. "Is this more tsai?" She took one out, turned it over to examine, and sniffed it.

Chu laughed, "No. That's argol. For fires."

"Is it grass, or what?" asked Lin.

"It's dried camel dung."

Lin replaced the argol brick, closed the bag, wiped her finger on it, and used the sleeve of her shirt to wipe her nose where the brick had lightly touched. "Camel patties, huh?"

The other cloth bag was the size of a football and Lin asked "What's in that bag? Or would I rather not know?"

"Bortz," Chu answered and pulled one out of the bag. It was dark brown, the size of a finger.

"It looks like a stick," said Vic. Her journal was out again and she made notes.

"It's dried meat," said Chu. "Grind it up, put the powder in water and use it to make stew or just drink it if you don't have anything else. It is for Narakaa, my wife."

Vic and Lin looked at each other and said, "Mongolian bouillon cubes!"

As they left the trading post, Vic asked, "What were your mother-in-law and her brother wearing?"

Chu's in-laws both wore clothing very similar, except for a bit of styling. It resembled a robe with a single button on one side, with a sash, and the billowing sleeves extended beyond the wearer's fingertips. The garment ended just below the knees and both Bayarmaa and Bat wore trousers beneath.

"It is called a deel," Chu told them. "It is the traditional dress. If you like I will have Narakaa make deels for you."

"Absolutely not!" said Vic. "Don't *have* your wife do anything. If she wants to teach Lin and me so we could make our own, that would be fun."

"Yes. You can make winter deels for it will be very cold while you are here."

Because of the late start from Dalan bulag they had less than three hours before sundown, however it didn't matter. There were things they wanted to do but no time schedule to keep. About half an hour before sundown, Chu pulled off the road and headed for some boulders at the bottom of a small hill. They were nearly there when a desert hare popped from behind a bush and darted. Vic saw it and stood up and pulled her revolver. Chu didn't get a chance to stop. Vic fired one shot and the hare jumped into the air, flipped and fell dead. Vic jumped out to retrieve the hare while Chu parked.

Lin pulled out some argol and started a fire. Vic cleaned the hare and in a few minutes it was roasting on a stick. While it cooked they set up their pup tents and put on jackets.

"How long before it begins to get really cold?" asked Vic.

"It would not be strange if you notice it is more cold every few days," Chu told her.

Later as they ate, the howls of wolves were heard in two directions. "Sounds like finding a wolf won't be a problem," said Vic.

The next morning they rose early and were eager. They continued northwest, more or less, with mountains in the near distance on their left. Around noon, Chu said he would cook them a traditional Mongolian meal to write about and diverged from the path toward some low hills. In the foothills, they came upon a colony of tarbagans and were able to shoot two before they dived into burrows.

"I will show you boodog," Chu told them. "They will soon begin to hibernate until Spring. You can make boodog with goat or other meat but I think tarbagan is best." They began a fire and dropped several stones into the flames. Chu showed them what wild onion looked like and Vic and Lin harvested wild onions for half an hour.

Back at the campsite, they found Chu removed the heads and organs and most hair from the tarbagans. He took salt from one of the "money" bags, and rubbed it inside of the carcasses. Then he put hot stones inside the bodies and closed them tight with leather cords.

The tarbagans were hung on branches over the fire for the outside to roast while the stones cooked the inside. The onions were put in water in their canteen cups and set on the fire. About half way through cooking, Chu opened the tarbagans to release steam, then resealed them. He warned that if steam wasn't released the boodog could explode.

About two hours after they began they enjoyed a meal of tarbagan boodog, very tender marmot meat with boiled onions. Vic and Lin loved it. The rest of the day was more of the same travel wise, as Vic made notes about boodog and asked Chu an unending stream of food related questions.

Chapter 6

Heaps of Corpses

Three hours out the next morning, soon after they passed a vast expanse of els on their right, Chu saw riders in the distance and alerted Vic and Lin.

When the riders neared, they could see there was no need for alarm. It was a man, his wife and two children, a boy and a girl each around 10. They led two pack horses.

Chu spoke with them for a while and Vic asked for and received permission to take a photo of the family. After she snapped two shots of the family she thanked them with a brick each of salt and tsai. Before the people rode on, Chu handed them a note, and said something which made the adults obviously happy.

When they were gone, Vic questioned, "What did you give them? They sure thought that paper was swell."

"A note to Bayarmaa and Bat. I asked them to help these people, just house their animals for awhile and let them work for anything they need."

"Aren't they nomadic? Don't they carry what they need," asked Lin.

"Usually, but they left Gazar quickly and abandoned some things. Red Beards were there two weeks past and a week ago a group of Russians came who may have been men of the Mad Baron. Both groups took whatever they wanted and killed several people. He and his family hid in the desert, but many things were taken from their ger. Then three days ago Mongolian soldiers came looking for Red Beards or the Russian bandits. There are several hundred camped outside the city and will likely stay awhile. The man was fearful for his wife and daughter, so they are going to Dalan bulag."

"That's terrible," said Lin. "You mean an entire town can be terrorized by group after group of thugs or whoever they call themselves?"

"Yes. Unfortunately, that is the way of life for now," answered Chu.

"How large is Gazar?" Vic asked.

"Ten times or more than Dalan bulag."

"Do we pass through it?"

"No, luckily. We would need to turn northward in a bit," Chu told her.

"Can we go there?" Vic asked. "Is it far?"

"Go to Gazar?" Chu looked unbelieving.

"Shouldn't it be fairly safe if the men there are Mongolian soldiers?"

86

"Maybe. Mongolia does not have an official army. It was disbanded by the Chinese last year. Groups have formed in anticipation of becoming a sovereign country again, but they are only as civil as the man who leads them."

Vic wanted to visit anyway, so a kilometer up the road they turned northeast and an hour before dark they ran into more people abandoning Gazar. This time three families traveled together and left for the same reason as the others. They told Chu he should stop because they couldn't reach Gazar before dark.

The soldiers were eager to find anyone associated with the Mad Baron or the Red Beards. The government decreed that every other ger must keep a fire burning throughout the night, and in every fifth ger someone must remain on watch all night. To attempt to enter Gazar after dark would probably get them all killed. They decided it would be prudent to camp early.

Mid-morning the next day they drove slowly into Gazar. Mongol soldiers were everywhere in groups of five or more. They all carried rifles with bayonets fixed and none of them looked friendly.

The people the night before told Chu an official office was set up in the center of town. "We will go there. It is best if we ask permission. We'll find who is in charge and I'll explain that you are a writer and want to take photos of Mongolian cities. If he says OK, we will take photos, if it isn't OK, we will quietly and quickly leave the way we came."

Vic said, "Sounds reasonable."

Shortly, they came to a long rectangular block building not unlike the trading post at Dalan bulag. At one end was an office.

Several soldiers stood outside the office door and Chu went up and spoke to them, and one of them went inside. After a few minutes, the man returned outside and spoke to Chu who waved for Vic and Lin to come up and the three of them followed the soldier inside.

An officer sat behind a desk and eyed them sternly as they entered. He didn't speak but looked intensely at Chu, and Chu, incidentally, looked as intensely at the officer. The officer stood and came around to face Chu eye to eye as they talked. It was evident that questions were asked, but Chu seemed to also be asking questions and the officer kept looking at Vic. Then the two men shook hands. The officer pointed to Vic and spoke to Chu and laughed. He held his arms open wide, like he might be telling about the big fish that got away.

Chu looked at Vic and Lin and said, "This is Captain Unegen. His brother and my father were very good friends and I met the captain once many years ago and he recognized me. What is more important, he recognizes Vic Challenger."

"What?" It still amazed Vic, but there was only one way. The picture and story of her and the jaguar in Mexico were syndicated worldwide. The captain read the story in a Russian paper.

"He is greatly surprised. He thought you would be bigger with massive muscles and maybe have a hairy face. He says you look too pretty to kill such a beast with only a knife."

For an instant, Vic was dumbfounded and showed it, then she smiled and said, "Thank him for the compliment and tell him I love his country."

Of course, Vic got to take photos. The captain personally escorted them throughout the town and Vic retold the story of Mexico through Chu, as she took photos of groups of soldiers and gers and camels. Late in the afternoon the captain took them to a field of what looked like large steamer trunks, each padlocked and with an oval slot on the side that was maybe 12 x 6 inches. Vic didn't count but there looked to be at least two dozen, and moans came from within several. With an ostentatious smile, the captain gestured and nodded toward the boxes and spoke.

Chu said, "He wants you to see how criminals are punished. Most will be in their box until they die."

Vic was horrified but managed a small smile and a slight nod as though she approved. She looked at Lin and saw she must be horrified, too, so she put a hand on Lin's shoulder and looked her in the eye and with a smile said, "We shouldn't show disapproval. We are his guests and they have a lot more guns. We can puke later," Vic finished as she gave the captain a smile and nod.

"Oh!" said Lin smiled and nodded as though she just understood something.

Chu translated that the captain invited Vic to take photos of their system. He thought it was more efficient as it didn't require as much space as a western jail and they did not feed those who committed the worst crimes, so money was saved because they would die before long to make room for other criminals. To further assure adequate punishment, prison boxes were designed too short and too low for the prisoner to either fully lie down or sit erect.

Vic snapped some photos and just before the third one, an old gray haired woman pushed her face and a forearm through the hole of her prison box, looked forlornly at Vic, and in the most lamentable voice Vic would ever hear, wailed in Mongolian and repeatedly curled her fingers in a gesture of need. Vic bit the inside of her cheek and took the photo, while in her mind she screamed, *what in the name of heaven could an old woman do, to deserve being starved to death in a box?* Vic and Lin were ready to leave.

The captain, however, suddenly became excited. Through Chu he told them an execution was scheduled for tomorrow but they could go ahead so Vic could witness it.

"Oh my God!" whispered Lin with a forced smile. "Are we going to watch them kill someone? What if it's that old woman? What if it's a child?"

Vic said, "Relax. We must continue to fake approval because there is nothing we can do," said Vic. "And it could be worse. He isn't going to execute someone just to make a show for us. He said they would be executed anyway and I am a reporter of sorts. We don't know the story behind any of the prisoners. Even the old woman may have murdered someone."

90

Chu agreed with Vic, but first told the captain they didn't want to change their rules or impose on the captain. The captain assured them, though, that it was no problem and afterward they could have dinner with him.

"Appetizing," said Lin.

Vic put an arm around Lin's shoulders and said, "It's just life, Lin. The very ugly side of life," and they both nodded at the captain and smiled.

Within minutes, a group of seven soldiers appeared and two prisoners were crudely yanked from their boxes and shoved out beyond the array of diminutive, solitary dungeons where they were forced to their knees with their backs to the town.

Vic asked why these two were being shot. One killed a Mongol soldier and the other gave information to Red Beards. The captain wanted to make an example. Vic looked at Lin and said, "Well, one is a murderer and the other committed treason. We would execute them in America, too, and certainly they knew their actions could get them killed."

There was no ceremony to the event. Once the men were on their knees, one soldier said something to the others, three soldiers aimed at the back of the head of each prisoner and then the one soldier spoke one word, *rener.* All six rifles went off. Three rounds from a high powered rifle didn't leave much and the two now almost headless corpses collapsed into the dirt. Then a soldier took each leg of the two and dragged them away. Vic snapped photos during the ordeal. Lin watched the execution with a strange fascination, but quickly looked away when a length of brain matter commenced to bounce along behind a corpse.

The captain smiled and said something to Chu who relayed to Vic, " He wants your opinion."

"Oh," said Vic, "It was so fast and efficient." As Chu translated, she nodded and smiled and so did Lin and the captain seemed quite pleased.

The sun was behind mountains and darkness was quickly descending. The captain now wanted to take them along to the outskirts of town where they hadn't been. Two soldiers went with them, and conspicuously kept their rifles at the ready. As they walked along in the general direction of the office but along the outside row of gers, in the deepening darkness they could just make out knee-high, irregular heaps of an unknown.

Then came low, vicious snarls and crunching sounds and the captain told the soldiers to shine lights toward the noise. The heaps were not stones or logs, as one might expect, but piles of corpses. There were old bones, half decomposed carcasses and newer dead. The source of the crunches and rips were wild dogs feeding on the carrion. They were not handsome, healthy dogs like Terkoz, but beasts half the size of Terkoz with conspicuous, weeping sores and missing large clumps of hair. Not one was without fresh or dried blood on its muzzle and yellow drool dripped from bared fangs.

The captain was proud of how the dogs were useful. The wind, most of the time, was from the other direction so people need not smell the dead and the dogs served a valuable service as they cleaned up well and even acted as sentries for that side of the town. Yet, he cautioned not to go in that area without a weapon. Just two nights before, one of his men went to urinate too near the dead without his weapon. Dogs attacked him and tore him to pieces. It was just at that exciting bit of information that fierce growls and snarls began near them, and the captain ordered the soldiers to shine their lights on the commotion. Several large, vicious dogs were ripping various body parts and chunks of meat from the two men just executed.

"I'm hungry," said Vic, "Can we go eat now?"

Chu told the captain what Vic said and he replied of course. Lin whispered, "I'm really not hungry but anything is better than seeing more, and after a second she added, "Does he really think we might want to go for a walk among piles of rotting dead people, whether we have a gun or not?"

Vic spoke to Lin quietly, "It's a horrible thing but this brutality has been around for 100,000 years and may well be here 100,000 years from now. Remind yourself it could be worse. We could be on the pile."

"That doesn't make it right," said Lin.

"Not to us, but it is his country, his culture, and in his way he is providing as much safety and civility to his people as he knows how. None of this is unusual for here and now. Even more important, you are a good person Lin. I know you will do good things in your life, good things

93

for others, good deeds that would go undone if you were on that pile. That is why we smile and nod. That makes it as close to right as it will ever get."

Back at the block building, they went into the trading post tavern beside the office. The couple who owned the business cleared a table and waited on the captain and his guests while the two soldiers who were with them through the revolting tour stood solemnly against the wall behind the captain.

They enjoyed the simple meal in spite of what they witnessed on the tour. They got all the boiled mutton and whole onions they wanted and drank tsai with milk and salt. During the meal Vic entertained the captain with stories of big game hunting in Africa and the earthquake. Then through Chu's translation she took notes about the captain's exploits and asked his permission to write about him, which seemed to please the captain greatly.

Afterwards, the captain offered the back of the restaurant for them to sleep. They thanked him and gladly accepted. Vic guessed the temperature outside hovered around 30 degrees Fahrenheit and it was windy.

Vic was about to go out for her sleeping roll when Chu stopped her and smiled at Lin and said, "Lin, you need to go get gear for all of us and seem pleasant about it."

"OK, I'm being pleasant," Lin replied and smiled. "Tell me why."

"The captain asked why you are with us, thinking you might be a spy for Red Beards. I told him you are from America also and that you

94

are Vic's servant. It seemed the most believable story for his ears," said Chu shrugging.

Lin continued to smile, nodded and when she spoke, Vic fought to keep from laughing. Since their days in high school, Lin practiced and became better and better at what she called her 'southern belle' accent. Vic loved it, but it always made her laugh. Unfortunately, Lin seldom used it unless she was upset.

Lin said, "Well now, I'll just take my little old self out there in the cold, the horrible cold, and fetch bed rolls for Master Chu and Lady Victoria as fast as this poor little servant girl can move. Thank you so much for the singular honor of waiting on the two of you. Did I mention the horrible cold? You all will pay tomorrow," she smiled and curtsied and started for the door. The captain said something and Lin heard Chu translate for Vic. "The captain says you have a very pleasant and obedient servant as befits a strong warrior." Vic struggled to hold in the laugh and thanked the captain through Chu and as she closed the door behind her, Lin made a sound quite similar to the growl of a wild, corpse-eating dog.

Despite the cordiality of the captain, the three slept lightly, each with a hand on the revolver beneath their shirt, but there was nothing to worry over. In the morning, after more boiled mutton for breakfast, they thanked the captain for his gracious hospitality and as Vic took a photo of the captain beside his horse, Chu disappeared inside for a moment. Just before they left, the captain spoke to Vic through Chu, "If you go west and high into the mountains you may find one of our leopards to fight or perhaps a bear, but if not, there are wolves everywhere. That would be a magnificent battle for you!"

Vic's answer was a big smile with much head nodding, "I would love to fight one of your wolves, maybe two at one time! Or even three!" Chu translated the intended exaggeration and it greatly excited the captain who told her he couldn't wait to see the photos in the newspaper.

Then they said goodbye and went out to the auto. When they climbed in, Vic and Lin found a new bag in the floor and asked Chu. He told them to ignore it. It was fabric for their deels. Mindful that the captain would force the shopkeepers to give it without pay, Chu paid for it while the captain was not around, and the owner of the shop dropped it in the auto.

They drove slowly out of town and then sped as much as they safely could, to put distance between them and Gazar.

"Chu," said Vic after they passed out of town, "Have you heard the expression *hell on earth*? I think that is where we spent the night."

"And how!" said Lin. "I see you have another small bag, Chu. What is it?"

"It's sweet aaruul." Chu dug in the bag as he drove and pulled one out. It looked a little like a white cookie, smooth, the size of a silver dollar. Aaruul turned out to be curdled milk that has been dried. It can be made of milk from pretty much any handy lactating animal and can be cut square or round in any size. It could also be run through a meat grinder to make worm aaruul. "We make our own but most times with salt and this has sugar. If made from mare's milk it is sweet by nature but we usually make it from sheep milk. The girls will like this."

"Original Mongolian candy," said Lin and Vic pulled out her journal to make notes.

After they traveled a few miles, Lin spoke again, this time in her southern belle accent.

"When we stop later, y'all eggs be sure and take it easy, find a place to put up your feet while I make everything ducky, like a good little servant. Maybe enjoy yourselves a nice little nap while I prepare your royal tsai and coffee. I wouldn't want either of you to break even a tiny little sweat. Maybe I can fetch a whole pack of wolves for Lady Victoria to fight!"

"I think we may be in for a hard time today if we don't do penance," Vic told Chu. When they stopped for lunch, Vic told Lin to crawl in the back seat where she could stretch out while Vic got a fire going and made Lin some tsai. It was about forty degrees so Vic pulled off her jacket, and laid it over Lin and asked if she was comfortable.

"Well that's right nice of you Missy Vic," said Lin and put her feet up on the back of the front seat to nap until the tsai was ready.

When they started off again, Vic asked Lin if they were square. "I guess that'll do," Lin answered without the southern belle touch.

By noon they turned back northwest, their route before they sidetracked to Gazar, and they covered about fifty miles before they stopped for the night.

Two days later in the early afternoon they ascended slowly, steadily up a long gentle slope into mountains. There was no road, merely some areas more sparse than others. They didn't climb to the top of the mountains. Chu turned to go along the contour of the mountain between stands of trees and suddenly topped a little rise and shouted, "There is my home!"

A hundred meters ahead was a ger like any other, but in a setting which made Vic and Lin both catch their breath. On three sides of this ger stood a beautiful patchwork of green pine, blue green spruce and the gray-brown orange of larch losing their leaves and behind it, rising above the trees, was a backdrop of distant, snow covered mountaintops. Chu honked the horn and yelled out in Mongolian. A woman came out and when she saw them she ran to meet the car and a little girl ran on either side of her.

Chapter 7

Wolves and Weapons

C hu stopped before the ger and jumped out and hugged his wife and lifted her off the ground while the two little girls wrapped their arms around his legs and squealed over and over, "Aav, Aav!" The four spoke Mongolian for several minutes, then Chu introduced his family to Vic and Lin.

His wife and daughters were quadrilingual, like Chu. They all spoke Mongolian, Chinese, and a little English and Russian. Of course, the girls spoke all four languages at a five year old level, which Vic liked since she knew zero Chinese, Mongolian or Russian.

The given name of Chu's wife was Narantsetseg, which means 'sunflower', but she was called Narakaa. The twin girls were Mönkhtsetseg, 'eternal flower' and Mönkh-Erdene, 'eternal jewel'. Luckily, like Narakaa they had shortened names or nicknames, Segree and Monkkaa. All three were excited to have visitors and the little girls immediately latched onto both visitors. They saw few Chinese other than their dad and never met a Westerner before Vic. Within a few minutes they named their new friends. They called Lin 'yanztai egch', nice big sister and Vic was 'yanztai bacgan', nice girl.

They stayed at the ger for several days for a fabulous vacation. Vic and Lin learned much of Mongolian fashion and cooking from Narakaa. Vic used several rolls of film to take photos of the mountains and the family. They both played often with the twins, but Lin especially enjoyed the little girls and they seemed to enjoy time with 'yanztai egch', since she spoke two of their languages.

A sizeable chunk of time was devoted to shagai or sheep ankle bones games. The twins taught them several shagai games, like cat's game, open catch, tossing three shagai, and four animals. Monkkaa or Segree always won. Vic was used to losing but Lin couldn't believe at first that five year olds were beating her in games. Lin did best in cat's game, a form of jacks or knucklebones.

Of course one big project was their deels. Narakaa guided them to cut and sew the fabric from Gazar. They used sheep skin to line the dels and two fabric knots served as buttons. The sleeves were fashioned longer than their arms to create overhang to keep hands warm when not using them. Slits were cut in the deel for mobility, especially on horseback, and Narakaa gave them silk sashes. Vic and Lin wondered why both front flaps of the deel folded completely across their body. When they added the sash they found a very handy pouch was formed above the sash between the folds.

Narakaa also helped them fashion the hides of sheep rear ends, turned inside out, into warm hats with ear flaps.

They went horseback riding with the entire family several times and on the first occasion they were astonished when Chu sat each girl up on her own horse and gave them the reins. They were excellent riders and Chu explained that all Mongolian children are taught to ride as soon as they can walk, if not sooner. At first Lin and Vic both were afraid the girls would fall on some of the slopes but on the second outing the girls said let's race so they did. The girls won and asked Chu why the nice girls couldn't ride better and Chu told the twins it was because they were not Mongolian. They thought that was funny and laughed until tears were in their eyes. They laughed so loud and long that Lin and Vic caught it and laughed until tears were in their eyes, too. Vic and Lin did not worry about the twins after that.

That night Vic borrowed a mirror from Narakaa and took the twins out to look at the moon. They positioned the mirror to catch the full moon reflection and used their magnifiers to view the lunar mountains and craters. Then Vic pointed out the asterism we call the Big Dipper and told about it and the legend of Calisto and Arcas. Then the twins, through Lin, told Vic and Lin about the Seven Gods, the very same set of stars. It was a very good night.

One day Vic and Lin played hide and seek with the twins in the forest beside the ger and Lin said, "Aren't they adorable. I can't get over them. When I look at them, I want to just pick them both

101

up and squeeze them!"

Vic said to Lin, "I would love to have a daughter someday, and laugh with her and watch her grow up. Of course, if I had a son, I would definitely not ignore him! I would love a son just as much."

"But a little Vic would be nice, huh," said Lin. "Dress her up with pretty dresses and a little cloche! I'd like to have a little Lin someday, too." Then Lin looked toward the woods where the twins were hiding and called out, "Here we come! Wǒmen shàngqián yǐ nǐmen!"

On the eighth day, they enjoyed an outing of sorts. The night before, a wolf killed a sheep and that was not a thing taken lightly. Wolves were like mortal and historic enemies of the Mongols. Sheep provided meat and milk and wool. Even more importantly, for a wolf to come so close was a danger to the girls. Chu kept dogs like all Mongols, but owned only two which were both killed a month earlier when they went into a herd of maral and were kicked to death. He didn't get a chance to replace them yet.

The wolf didn't chew on the entire sheep, so a hind leg and the head were kept to eat later. Chu took the rest to lure the wolf.

Narakaa followed a pair of wolves a couple of times, but lost them, yet she had a good idea where they might be. They went down in a valley about two miles from their ger. Several openings were obvious on the far side of the valley on a steep hillside. Chu left the others a good distance from the slope behind some cover and rode over to drop the bag with the carcass below the openings, then rode in a circle back to join the others. He said there were tracks where he dropped the bait and they settled where they could observe unseen.

Chu said Vic or Lin could shoot the wolf if it came out but they both declined because Narakaa said she wanted to kill this wolf. They could go on a hunt another day.

The twins amazed Vic and Lin. Neither ever saw five year olds so quiet. They didn't make a sound as they intently and patiently peered through the bushes for the wolf. An uneventful hour of watching ended when Monkkaa waved a hand and got their attention, "Psst! " Then she and Segree both whispered, " Chinua!" Of course, Vic and Lin were impressed about one second later when they saw the muzzle of a wolf inch out from a dark hole on the slope.

Earlier, Narakaa drove a long branch with a fork in the end into the ground with the fork at eye level. She now placed the barrel of her rifle in the fork and took aim. Then she relaxed and raised the barrel a bit. "There is another," she said to Lin in Chinese and immediately another wolf came out and the two animals sniffed the air for a sign of danger.

Narakaa spoke to Lin in Chinese and nodded right. Then she re-aimed on the post and Lin aimed without a post. For a few seconds it seemed no one breathed, then Narakaa whispered "Rener." Simultaneously the two rifles fired and both wolves lurched just slightly and fell over. The twins immediately jumped up and down and clapped their hands and jabbered rapid fire in their mix of Mongolian, Chinese, Russian and English.

103

They all led their horses over to the wolves and Lin and Narakaa each pulled a knife to skin the wolf she shot. The wolves were on a ledge about six meters up and Chu climbed up and threw the bodies down. Both pelts were a beautiful bushy mix of dark gray to silver on the back and sides, with pure white bellies. The twins ran to watch Lin and almost immediately tapped her on the arm and shook their heads. They spoke in Chinese, obviously to condemn Lin's technique.

Vic looked up at the hillside which went almost perpendicular to the ground from just above the lair. There was practically no vegetation on the hill and Vic said "These barren hills are beautiful. I think I'll have a look around."

Lin fought to not laugh as the twins continued to scold her. Vic looked over and said "I just can't bear to witness the humiliation!" Then she laid her carbine down, pulled up the sleeves of her deel, tightened the straps on her pack and scaled the steep hill without hesitation. Her five companions stopped what they were doing and watched Vic pull herself up the cliff as nimbly as a rock squirrel. Vic came to the ledge a good 25 meters above them and went out of sight and the others went back to skinning the wolves.

Three hours later when the wolves were skinned and their meat cut for food, Vic had not yet returned, so Lin moved to where she could see the ledge. Vic sat admiring the valley and Lin called to her twice before Vic looked down and waved and scrambled down the cliff.

When Vic reached the bottom she smiled and told them "I got some great photos and wrote some terrific descriptions, if I do say so myself. I also took on a bit of cargo up top," and with a twinkle in her eye, she opened her pack and pulled out the bounty. "Look what I found!"

"That's jade! " said Lin.

"I'm going to make a knife!"

"A stone knife like you used to battle the jaguar?" Chu asked. Vic told him yes and Chu translated for his wife and she suddenly seemed very excited. "Narakaa wants to know if you will make her a knife?" Chu told Vic.

Vic looked at Narakaa and nodded. Then, with just her empty haversack, she started back up the cliff face to collect more jade. As she topped the edge to the ledge, Lin yelled up to her, "Get enough for me, too! And for Chu." When Vic came down, she said she brought enough for the girls, too. Then she went to what was left of the skinned wolf carcasses and cut the ligaments from their legs. Then they returned home where the wolf hides were stretched on frames atop the ger.

The next morning after breakfast Lin and Narakaa took down the wolf hides and crumpled them to keep them soft, then turned and re-stretched them and returned them to the ger roof. Then they began work on their knives. First they collected tools - a hammer stone, points from maral antlers for a pointed tool, sheep skulls full of sand and fine gravel for sharpening and a pad of camel leather to lay across their lap for a work surface.

Each began with a block of jade larger than the knives which would be the finished product. Then under Vic's direction they plunged into the slow, careful process and with angled, almost delicate

105

strikes, began to shape their new weapons from the raw, green stones.

After sunset on the fourth day, they wrapped the flat end of their stone knives with camel leather and all were happy with their jade knife, especially Segree and Monkkaa.

The following day, everyone else went to other activities and Vic pulled out the largest stone she collected and began to work on an ax head. It would not be as large as she liked, but it would be deadly and it would be beautiful. Vic planned to shape and sharpen only one side. She needed to find a suitable haft and shape and harden it to take the stone, and then shape the back of the stone head for a good fit. She would then slowly scrape and grind furrows into the stone for her cordage. After sundown on the sixth day of her labor, Vic used the wolf sinew and pine resin to attach the head to the haft.

Vic told the others she regretted she was so absorbed for so long, but no one minded. For Vic, no matter what other weapons were available, she felt unarmed without a war ax. Now Vic was armed.

After the evening meal on the day Vic finished her ax, what seemed to have become an obligatory part of her life happened again. Vic was asked to tell the jaguar story. Narakaa thought her twins would love to hear the story told by Vic herself, and when the girls clapped it was inescapable.

To begin, Chu described a jaguar to the twins and told them how big it was. Vic thought, from the way Chu spread his arms that he might be exaggerating the size of the cat. When he held his hands apart to illustrate the size of the fangs, she smiled. Chu seemed to be describing a saber-cat.

When Vic finished the story of the jaguar, the twins bounced and laughed and asked their mother questions, then clapped at the answers. It made Vic feel so good to see their excitement that she thought that if she came all this way just for this night, the trip would be worth it. Then the night got even better.

While the twins bounced and laughed, Lin leaned toward Vic and whispered, "When are you going to tell me the rest of the story? Don't forget."

At the same time, Narakaa spoke to Chu and then he translated, "Narakaa thanks you. Because of stories like yours, she knows her daughters will grow to be great women."

Vic froze at those words. In Mexico, Pablo spoke those exact words about his nieces just before he died. For a second Vic stared silently at Narakaa. "Tell Narakaa that she is a wonderful mother and that I hope someday I may be a mother as fine as her. I am honored to share the story with her and her daughters and I know they will be great women, but it will be because they have a strong kheezh."

Narakaa smiled back at Vic and nodded at the translation. For a moment everyone was silent. Vic looked at Lin then at Chu then at the twins and Narakaa then back at Lin. "Would all of you care to hear the rest of the story? The parts no one knows except those who were there. The secret story. It will take a while and it is late but if you want to hear it I will tell it."

Chu translated for Narakaa as Vic spoke and no sooner did Vic finish when Narakaa nodded and the twins did their clap, laugh and bounce

107

again. Then the twins positioned themselves cross-legged in front of Vic with a beautiful look of childish wonder on their faces.

"Tell us Vic," said Lin.

So Vic told more of the story. The jaguar didn't just wander into camp but was attracted by Pablo's body. She told of the gunfight where Pablo was killed. "That's where I met O and JJ," she told Lin.

Vic told them about being taken by what the camp cook Maria called a thunderbird, and how she later killed the beast in the underground river.

When Vic stopped, Narakaa spoke and Chu told her "Narakaa thinks there is more. You were in that jungle for a greater purpose."

"Narakaa is wise," Vic said. Then she looked at Lin and half whispered, "Here's the scary part, where you might think I'm a fruitcake." Lin shook her head and said, "No way."

Then Vic told the secret story of Africa, the years of vivid dreams, the earthquake, and how she fainted and in the space of three minutes she re-experienced her last weeks as Nat-ul. She told of Nu, and how he killed Gr for her. Finally she told how she visited the cave re-opened by the earthquake, where Nu died as he protected the head of Gr for Nat-ul. Then she said aloud what she had never spoken aloud before. Until that moment the thought lived privately in her mind. "I loved Nu above all else and I still do. We were buried by earth and swallowed by sea and yet the love lives, and I will search for Nu until I find him, or until death stops me again."

When Vic finished, Narakaa and Lin thanked her for sharing her secret story and the twins hugged her.

Nor did a single one of them harbor any measure of doubt of the story and accepted it as readily as if Vic told them she walked in a Nebraska cornfield. Nor did Vic feel any discomfort at sharing her secret with those present as she feared beforehand.

In the morning as they were waking, Lin grabbed Vic's arm and shook her, "Hey. I don't think you're a fruit cake. I'm glad I know why you want to visit these wild and wooly places. I want to keep traveling with you, too. Maybe I will be in the right place at the right time like you and will remember something wonderful."

"Thanks Lin. You have an open invitation!"

They were at the ger twelve more days. They took several day rides and were amazed at the array of wildlife. They saw a rare mazalai or Gobi's brown bear, lynx, saïga antelope, zeer, wild donkey, wild camel, and argali sheep. On one ride they spotted a small herd of takhi or Przewalski horses. Vic snapped the first photos about 800 meters distant, and stopped to take another photo every 200 meters. The takhi finally trotted off when they were about 100 meters away.

On one day trip Vic shot a lynx and on another Lin shot a fox. They used those skins for the outside of their sheep butt hats which made them warmer and quite attractive enough to wear anywhere.

Vic wrote a lot in her journal, she and Lin taught the twins more English and learned some Mongolian from them and both learned more about daily life in Mongolia and reveled in playing shagai games with Monkkaa and Segree, although they continued to lose.

One morning Lin said exactly what Vic was

thinking, "Could heaven be any better? A loving, happy family and scenery so fresh and beautiful it excites and amazes you all over again every morning. Mongolia is magnificent!"

Chapter 8

Monsters and Bad Guys

Then Chu was ready to take them to see the primitive rock paintings. They hoped also to see maral and Vic still wanted a wolf. They took horses this trip and waved goodbye to the twins and Narakaa just as the sun peeked over the left shoulder of the alpine ger home.

It was noticeably colder as Chu predicted. Days were generally no warmer than the mid-thirties and nights were near zero Fahrenheit. Heavy trousers and flannel shirts under the dels kept them warm while they were active and Chu gave each a sheep skin to add to her bedroll for ground cover.

They took it slow down the mountain. When they reached the steppes, they headed toward another mountain range. Chu timed it well and before dark they came to what Chu called a river, but Vic and Lin called it a creek. It was about fifty meters across but no deeper than a foot at that point. Just a few meters on the other side of the river were dunes, the els. There were some trees and boulders to break the icy wind which gusted down from the northeast so that is where they set up camp.

By the time the sun was completely up, they broke camp, had coffee and dried mutton, crossed the river, and headed out onto the els. The campsite was lost behind a dune within minutes and all they could see in every direction was sand. There were no plants nor even rocks. Just sand. Of course, Vic stopped to snap photos.

Chu told them, "I've been across the els often and can usually travel a straight line by watching the sun move. It is important to keep a straight line. These els are not that wide. Perhaps only eight kilometers here. But the length is great. They stretch 100 kilometers north toward the mountains. If you lost direction and went the length, you could run out of food and water and die. The shortest distance across these els is to the northeast or southwest, give or take."

They were twenty-five minutes or so into the ride, probably half way across the els when Chu halted his horse and pointed to a half dozen small trees to their right, a miniature, scraggly oasis in the midst of thousands of square kilometers of uninterrupted sand. "Let me show you something useful," Chu said and headed toward the trees.

"We've seen these before," said Lin.

"A few times," said Vic. "We camped beside some the first night out of Kalgan."

"It is an important plant on the steppes and in the els. It can save your life and now you shall learn about it."

The site included a couple of patches of semi hard surface where the sand was packed and was

112

like a crust. The three dismounted and Chu stood beside one of the shrubs. "This is a zag tree. It is called saxaul tree by foreigners. It can save your life, " said Chu and broke off a branch that appeared to be dry and peeled a strip of bark. Then he tipped his head back, squeezed the bark and water dripped into his mouth.

"Almost like the lianas in a jungle," said Vic.

"When the bark or a limb is dry it is good for a fire." Chu bent down and cleared sand from a root, cut it and pulled it from the ground. What looked like small potatoes grew along the root. "These are not part of the tree. This is cistanche." Then Chu spoke to Lin in Chinese. Lin seemed excited and the two spoke Chinese for a minute, then Lin turned to Vic.

"Cistanche is an herb used in Chinese medicine. I use it a lot but I've never seen it like this. We get it in jars imported to us. Chu, could I grow it if I took some home?"

"I don't know, but my guess is they would grow. They are very hardy. " said Chu. Then he quickly added, "Wait, you need a zag tree, too, I think. But maybe a zag root will grow you a tree."

"Oh," said Lin. "Worth trying I guess. This is great stuff, Vic," and Lin placed the cistanche and the saxaul root in her pack. Vic snapped photos of the tree and of Lin as she cut a root, then replaced her camera into her pack.

In spite of the temperature, the sun warmed them up in their dels and it was bright. Lin said, "Makes a nice shade tree, too." She dropped hard in the shadow of a zag tree and immediately stared up at Vic with a look of bewilderment.

"This doesn't feel right," Lin said as she pressed on the sand.

Under Lin, the ground seemed to move and suddenly from a foot beside her, the sand exploded upward and the most bizarre and horrid creature any of the three could imagine reared up a meter high beside Lin!

Vic had no idea what it was, but it opened a mouth armed with multiple rows of pointy teeth and was large enough to easily gulp Lin's head. The mouth reminded her of a lamprey and she didn't wait to see what it would do. Making perhaps the fastest draw of her life, to date, Vic pulled the revolver from her deel sash and from the hip put three rounds into the cavernous mouth. Meanwhile, Lin rolled to the side and jumped up. Her revolver was in her hand by the time she was on her feet!

"Holy jumping Jehoshaphat," Lin cried. "What is that thing?"

"I don't believe it! Watch for more," Chu said as he warily looked all around them.

"That must be a death worm. I thought it was just legend," Chu told them. "All my life I've heard stories about these creatures. When people disappear in the desert, it is always said the death worms got them, but no one ever produced a body."

Vic and Lin kneeled down beside the thing which was only partially visible. It was obvious that much more of it was still underground and they guessed it must be at least two meters long. The teeth were not large. The longest were in the first row and only about an inch long. They both poked the body and agreed it felt spongy but firm, a bit like a giant caterpillar.

114

The body was thick and muscular, dark red and segmented with smooth scales. "For all the world, this looks like a gut," said Vic.

"Olgoi-Khorkhoi," said Chu, "Mongolian for intestine worm. Russians and other foreigners originated the term death worm."

Then Chu cautioned them. "Be careful you two. The stories say that they can shoot a death ray but descriptions sound like an electrical charge. They are also said to spit poison that kills instantly and dissolves the victim."

"What a useful pet," said Lin. "It could dissolve your garbage, control the mice, probably till your garden and be a guard dog."

On either side of the grotesque mouth was a horizontal situated pincer. Vic slipped on gloves and pulled the pincer nearest her. "Look at this," she said. "Look how it twists!"

"A mandible!" cried Lin excitedly. "A pair of mandibles! And they can be manipulated to grab you any way you turn." Vic twisted the mandible ninety degrees both right and left.

"The inside edge is like a razor and the tip is sharp," Vic noted. "They can be used to stab and hold prey or slice it in two!"

"How many ways could this thing kill you?" asked Chu. "Electrocute you, dissolve you, slice you in half, impale you or chew you up!"

"One's all it takes," said Vic as she allowed the mandible to fall shut. "This is big enough to easily take your head off, Lin."

Lin replied, "I'd rather not think about that. Whew, what a stink! Reminds me of working with acids."

"Yes. Plus a stench like rotten eggs and a little like something dead," said Vic.

"An unsavory mix," said Chu, "and I think it is fast growing stronger."

Vic picked up a dry branch and poked at the carcass again. It was no longer spongy and firm. When Vic prodded, the branch penetrated the skin easily and a yellow green sludge ran out and the horrible stench doubled! Immediately the branch began to dissolve where the odious mess touched it. Vic dropped the stick and she and Lin stood and stepped back. "Maybe we should leave," Vic said.

"We probably should leave quickly," said Chu. "Look!"

Vic and Lin looked toward the dunes where Chu pointed. The sand undulated in several places, as several large unknowns wriggled toward them just beneath the surface.

They kept their eyes on the movement below the sand as they backed to the horses. The horses were already jittery and needed no prodding to begin a gallop. They glanced behind and eyed the sand around them as they went, but galloped for only a couple of minutes.

Then Chu slowed and turned them at a right angle. "We are probably OK, now," he said. "Let's continue to the canyon."

"Well, Chu, you may be the only person in Mongolia who can tell why no one has ever produced evidence of a death worm," said Vic.

Lin added, "Even if the worm doesn't eat everything that goo dissolves victims to nothing and if you kill one it dissolves itself before you can show anyone." Then to Vic she said, "You didn't

116

get to take a photo. Show the world!"

Vic shook her head, "That's OK. It would be like a thunderbird."

"You think no one would believe, even a photo?" Lin asked.

"What would you think if someone you didn't know showed you a photograph of a creature unlike anything you have ever seen, described what you saw back there and told you all physical evidence conveniently dissolved?"

"I think in Mongolia people would believe," said Chu.

"Maybe they would," Vic said, "but I need to remain credible to readers in Nebraska first and foremost, so I can have a job that pays my way to places like this. I have seen enough strange things I could believe it, but most people have no experience with such oddities, but they have heard of P.T. Barnum. They wouldn't believe a poison spitting, electric worm as big as a man with a mouth like a lamprey and looks like a pig gut and dissolves itself if you kill it. I just saw it and I'd have a hard time believing what I just said."

In another half hour they were across those els which represented only a fraction of the vast region known as the Gobi. They were on harder ground, a Mongolian prairie, with many zag trees and other small plants.

Half a kilometer ahead the mouth of a canyon was visible at the foot of barren hills and Chu thought it was the canyon they came to see. Chu told them it was only about 120 meters deep and very rocky, so they left their horses at the twenty-meter-wide mouth. Even from the entry to

117

the canyon they could see what they came for. They walked almost to the canyon's far end where primitive animals and stick-like people were painted on the canyon wall about five meters above ground.

"How or why did they make drawings that high up?" asked Chu.

Lin asked, "You read up on this, Vic. What's the answer?"

"They probably didn't. These were likely made at least a hundred thousand years ago and it could have been a million years ago. It may not rain much here, but over that span of time, there has been enough wind and rain to wear away the valley floor until it is five meters lower than when the drawings were made."

"So the cave dwellers just stood and drew these where it was easy to reach," said Lin.

Vic replied, "Yes. The back wall may have been right here at one time and has been eroded back five meters. This was probably a ravine and this was probably the end. It was higher and there may have been a cave here. Over time, nature, wind and rain, eroded the ravine and dug this canyon."

As she spoke Vic took off her pack and brought out her camera. She opened it up and snapped photos of the paintings and one of Lin and Chu below them. Then Lin snapped a photo of Vic looking up at the primitive art.

Unknown to the three, they were not quite alone. As they approached and entered the canyon, they were intent on the goal and still talked about the death worms, so they did not notice the men who moved in the shadow of the mountain three quarters of a kilometer distant. The men noticed the three on the open sands, however, and halted, dropped and watched.

Vic just secured her camera in the pack when she felt a chill up her spine and her neck hair stood. Before she could look around or question it, a Chinese voice called out from behind them. Startled, the three looked toward the canyon mouth and pretty much stopped breathing for a moment. Spread the width of the canyon were Chinese men in various forms of dress, thirty across and four deep, all armed. "Red Beards," whispered Chu.

"How did we let ourselves get into this?" whispered Vic.

"What do we do?" asked Lin.

The man who appeared in charge yelled again.

"He wants to know if you are Russian, Vic," said Chu.

Vic smiled and called out "We are Americans from the United States."

Eyes only, Vic quickly survey the area.

The commander impatiently yelled again.

"He wants us to drop our guns and go to him," Chu translated for Vic.

"Would that be a good idea?" asked Lin.

"Feels like a very bad idea," said Vic, "but so does a shootout. What do you think Chu?"

"If we don't drop our guns they will probably shoot us in about one minute. If we drop them they will probably torture us and then shoot us."

As they pondered their dilemma and Vic sought a plan, the trio continued to nod and smile as a stall, but suddenly the Chinese commander shouted and the first row of men raised their rifles and took aim!

There was no more time to think about it. Vic

continued to nod and smile and whispered, "When I say jump, dive behind a rock, but don't start to shoot until you hear them coming. Jump!"

There were plenty of large boulders. Lin and Chu held their carbines in their hands and dived behind different man-high stones. Vic's carbine leaned against another boulder. She grabbed her weapon and dropped behind that cover.

As they dove for cover, thirty rifles from the front row of Red Beards fired! Then fired again. Then again. For a moment there was silence.

"Hey Vic, how about a little warning before you say jump right now," called Chu.

"Wasn't time." Vic was listening for the sound of men coming for them but there was no sound. Then the commander yelled out again.

"Holy crap!" said Lin.

"What did he say?" asked Vic.

Chu answered, "He says if we come out he will kill us quick without pain. If he is forced to come get us he will cause us great suffering."

Vic said, "Don't try to stand up, you'll just die. Shoot at the boulders in the walls of the canyon, a side each. The bullets will ricochet. Fire about every two seconds and alternate shots. That may keep them from rushing us immediately and will help conserve ammunition. I'm going to shoot at the top."

"The top?" Chu and Lin both wondered aloud.

"Start shooting," said Vic and rolled to position herself with a view of the top of the canyon at the point where she last saw the soldiers.

The Red Beards were still in the general location but were now crouched and tried to ricochet their shots the way Chu and Lin were, but it wasn't working. The three were too near the end wall of the canyon so the angle put the enemy bullets into the canyon wall behind them.

Vic's target was a boulder with a good four meter diameter which jutted out at least ten meters, perched precariously seventy five meters above the soldiers. Where that immense boulder met the cliff face was dirt. A one meter stone jutted out from the dirt wall below it as though it might be the one thing holding the enormous boulder in place. Vic hoped the top gargantuan rock was cantilevered over the small one and not part of an even larger formation stretching back into the canyon wall. She felt there was a pretty good chance since the entire canyon floor seemed to be a debris field of loose dirt and stone washed from higher up the mountain over the millennia.

Vic emptied her carbine into a spot at the base of the smaller stone, then reloaded and emptied it again. Then she reloaded again. Lin and Chu continued to alternate their shots and fired every few seconds. The Red Beards fired little more, an indication of the value of ammunition.

"OK," Vic said, "Here's my plan for what it is. If I can cause a landslide it should cause enough distraction for me to get up this wall. I can work my way to the canyon mouth. These guys had to come on horses. If I can get to the horses and stampede them into the canyon, there will be a lot of confusion and dust. I will bring our horses behind the stampede and we can ride off into the sunset. I know it sounds a little lame, but you two can't climb the wall and if they charge we couldn't shoot and reload fast enough. Any better ideas?"

Chu just said no, Lin said, "I don't like it but I can't think of anything else."

A half dozen times they heard the cry of someone hit by a shot from Chu or Lin, but the didn't hear the two men who belly crawled to them until they suddenly sprang over the boulders!

Vic jerked to one side and and a bullet from one Red Beard tore up dirt where her head lay a second before as a bullet from Vic hit the man in the center of his chest.

Lin and Chu both fell sideways and the other Red Beard blasted the hard ground between them as they both put a bullet in his gut. Immediately they rolled back in place and resumed their measured firing.

Vic was back shooting at the rock and her shots were having an effect. Large clumps of dirt fell from below the smaller rock and first the smaller and then the huge boulder tilted. The Red Beards began to yell excitedly and Chu called over to Vic, "They see what you are doing! They will either run away or charge us."

Vic yelled back, "I'll put my money on a charge. You'll need to take a chance. If they sound like they're coming this way, get prone and shoot from around the boulder at ground level. You'll be less of a target. Lin, you're good with either hand so every couple of shots switch sides, to keep them guessing where to shoot."

It all happened at once.

The Red Beards charged so Lin and Chu dropped and began direct fire and neither wasted a bullet.

Vic continued firing as she spoke and now the bottom smaller boulder broke loose and rolled down taking a huge amount of dirt with it.

The large boulder tilted downward more at the same time which caused the Red Beards to pause and look up with apprehension. For one second nothing moved, then a massive volume of dirt was displaced below the gigantic boulder and it broke free and half slid and half rolled toward the canyon floor. It brought with it rocks and dirt and boulders which were one and two meters across. Easily enough debris to fill a dozen box cars rolled down and across the canyon.

Vic rose and moved over to fire at the Red Beards, but there was no need. Maybe half the Red Beards were under the collapse and most of the remaining men ran the other direction. Lin and Chu finished the only six on their side of the collapse.

Vic didn't wait for the dust to settle, but called, "Let's go!" Then she jerked up her pack and slung it on as she ran toward the collapse with Lin and Chu beside her. "That was more of a landslide than I expected. Let's see if we can all slip by in the dust and confusion," Vic told them as they ran.

The cliff side collapsed and rolled across the little canyon floor to the opposite side which created a wall that split the canyon in two. The new wall was an arc of stones and debris highest at the wall that buckled. Against the far wall the debris was only about two meters high so escape was not a problem. The three were at the barrier of fallen debris when they came to a sudden stop.

Zt. Zt. Zt. "What's that?" Lin questioned.

Suddenly it sounded as though every surviving Red Beard began to fire at once.

Zt. Then the screams began. A second later they heard an explosion. "They have grenades," said Chu.

123

"But they are not throwing them at us and who are they shooting at? "   As they took a step backwards the three heard stones falling to their left. The air was clear enough they saw a bulge push out of the canyon wall and slide-roll along the column of debris.

The ball was writhing and began to disjoin into dozens of death worms! Most were a good three meters long with a diameter as great as a man. The screams and explosions seemed to have attracted them for every worm moved away to the other side of the debris.

The three continued backwards, eyes always to the front and the worms.

"I think you opened a nest," said Chu.

"Or in this case, it looks like that can of worms I'm always hearing about," said Lin.

Zt. Zt. The sound repeated every few seconds. Another grenade exploded and the tortured screams continued. "I hate to do nothing. They may have been fighting us but at least they are human," said Vic. As she finished speaking, two of the Red Beards came running across the top of the collapse. Later the three recalled what they saw and each bore the same nightmare mental image. The faces of the two men were twisted in anguished terror as though they fled demons from hell!

The ground sprayed up to one side of the two, a worm reared up and *Zt,* from the small hole above the mouth came a yellow-white flash of light. It flared to the nearest man, who fell dead, and the three no longer wondered about the sound. The other Red Beard halted and fired. The head of the thing splattered but the man halted at a price. Behind him, another worm burst from the dirt, closed the deadly mandibles around the man's middle, and sliced him in two. The extreme horror on his face before, was nothing compared to the look on his face as he attempted futilely to hold his intestines from spilling out as his torso and lower body fell in opposite directions. There was a single scream as the worm fell on the man to feed.

Vic's eyes narrowed and she growled. "Whether we can help them or not, we'll be trapped if we don't move. The chance to get out of here will not improve." Vic ran to the right edge of the collapse and pulled herself up, with Lin and Chu just behind.

As she passed near the feasting worm, Vic blew the creature's brains out. Worms burst up from the ground twice before they dropped to the other side of the debris wall, but the reflexes of the three were so adrenaline super charged that each worm died from three bullets at almost the instant it emerged.

When they dropped to the other side they stopped, mesmerized for just a moment by the sight. Only six Red Beards remained of the original hundred plus, and they were in a circle, back to back. Each yelled in desperation and fired or clubbed worms with an empty rifle. All around were dead worms stacked one on the other, dozens of them, yet still more slithered down the hill and others popped up from the earth.

"There is no way we can help them, Vic," said Chu. In the time Chu spoke another Red Beard fell to the electric charge of a worm, as a comrade lost a leg to the mandibles of a worm which came from the ground.

"I know," said Vic simply and ran toward the mouth of the canyon along the wall on the far side from the collapse. Although it would not save the men, Vic still fired as they passed. She dropped three worms and Lin and Chu followed Vic's example and brought down a couple each.

When the three came out of the canyon they found four horses of the Red Beards partly eaten and that told the story. Worms came up outside the canyon, too, and those horses were killed before they could bolt. The rest dashed into the desert or along the mountain. Chu's horses were well trained, however, and wouldn't go far. In short order he spied them a few dozen meters into the desert and yelled out to them. Obediently the horses came at a gallop, but there were only two horses, Chu's and Lin's.

As the two horses approached, a worm burst out of the ground between the three and the horses. Lin shot it dead but the horses stopped, neighed and shuffled and wouldn't come closer. Lin and Chu ran toward the horses, but Vic scaled boulders beside the canyon mouth and climbed to a height of six meters, well out of range of an electric charge.

Lin and Chu mounted before Lin noticed Vic wasn't with them, and yelled back at her, "Vic! What are you doing? Come on. We can both ride this horse."

"No!" yelled Vic as another worm burst from the ground. Chu shot it dead before it could emit a charge, but both horses reared and were difficult to hold in place. "Go before a worm injures a horse or one of you. I'm OK up here. There are horses loose

126

all along the mountainside. When things quiet down, I'll catch up with one and then catch up to you. I'll meet you later across the river where we camped before. It's too dangerous to do anything else right now. You two need to get out of the area! I'm OK Lin, go!" As though to emphasize the danger, another worm burst from the ground and pelted Lin and Chu with dirt before Lin put two rounds in it. The horses reared as two worms came squirming out of the canyon and something moved under the dirt near them,

"Ok," Lin yelled unconvincingly. "Hurry and find a horse, Vic! I won't budge from camp until you get there!" Then Lin and Chu turned their mounts and galloped away.

127

VIC: MONGOL

Chapter 9

Exploding Mountain

Vic watched them disappear quickly into the sun's glare on the white sand. Then she dropped her pack on top of the boulder in the clear *just in case* and propped her carbine against it.

Then she took extra cartridges for her revolver from the pack and stuffed them in her deel pouch. Armed with her revolver, stone knife and war ax, Vic then scurried up the cliff to where she could walk back and look down into the canyon. There were no more screams, no more humans standing. The worms feasted and from even 30 meters above Vic could hear flesh sucked from bones and the bones crushed in mandibles.

Vic found a place where a tremendous slab was pushed up in ages past to form a diagonal trail to the floor of the canyon, at least it made a trail for Vic. Another modern might find it difficult to lend the name trail to what Vic looked down upon.

It was mostly smooth rock sloped at a thirty-five degree angle and but a foot wide. Below were large boulders and jagged rocks that would surely kill anyone who fell more a couple of meters. A fall from any height might leave one helpless until the worms came to feed.

With her back against the wall, Vic side-stepped down the ledge and stopped at the same level as the opened nest across the canyon. She had a good view of the three-meter-high tunnel situated about five meters above the canyon floor. Vic watched, safe from a charge at that height and if she didn't move, they probably would not notice her while they fed.

The scene below Vic was nightmarish, with dismembered, partially eaten corpses everywhere. Detached hands seemed to grasp futilely for some support to pull them from the hell of this day. There were many more dead worms than Red Beards and all were quickly dissolving into the transparent, putrescent sludge.

Vic watched the charnel feast for a minute and noticed that the worms, as they got their fill of flesh, slithered slowly up the side of the collapse and entered the opened tunnel.

The first thing Vic wanted to do was venture down to the canyon floor and collect ammunition. The Red Beards used a hodge-podge of weapons. She didn't expect any of the unusual .351 carbines but sighted several .45's. If they got in another jam, especially if it was close quarters, more ammo for the revolvers would be welcomed. It wouldn't hurt to have a few grenades, either.

Vic looked for the nearest pack, and spied one

whose straps were held tight by the severed forearm and hand of a Red Beard, just half a dozen steps from the wall and almost directly below her. She didn't need to consider it. The moment she saw the pack she ran down the few meters to the floor, revolver in hand, dashed for the pack, scooped it up, slung it over her shoulder, and retreated to the wall and up the ledge again. When she stopped, she saw that her foray seemed to go unnoticed.

Vic pried the fingers from the strap and dropped the hand to the canyon floor then looked inside the pack. It held one grenade, perhaps two dozen loose cartridges that looked like .38's and other things of no value to them. Vic dumped all but the grenade. She then took a quick survey below for grenades or cartridges loose on the ground. She spotted two loose grenades and three cartridge belts. Those would be first. Then she would need to take time to look in packs.

After six forays to the canyon floor, Vic improved their supplies by at least 200 rounds of .45 ammo and four grenades. By then, perhaps half the worms were returned to the tunnel and those that remained continued to gorge, so Vic jumped to the floor of the canyon and loped through the carnage for the seventh time. With the swiftness of a deer fleeing the wolf, she dashed from pack to pack and searched.

As she rummaged the fourth pack, a worm noticed her. Vic pulled her ax and swung it to slice half way through the worm's body below the head. Then she bent down to clean the stone in the sand. While she wiped the caustic blood from the ax another worm came toward her so she blew its

131

brains out, then another worm reared up in front of her. She shot it dead, too, but now several others were headed her way, so Vic retreated toward the ledge in a zig zag. Enroute, she twice jumped widening streams of the acidic sludge and shot a worm that burst up from beneath a pile of corpses. However, as she traversed that gauntlet she was able to scoop up six more packs before she retreated up the ledge laden with at least sixty pounds of unknown plunder.

One by one Vic opened the packs and found a bonanza. Two climbing ropes, at least two hundred more .45 cartridges and a dozen grenades! Vic looked back into the canyon which was fast transforming into a shallow pond of disgusting putrescence from which the fetid odor rose even to where she stood. With little conscious thought, Vic looked across at the tunnel entrance, a plan crystallized, and she thought *We won't need all these grenades.*

At the level where she stood, Vic was able to circle the canyon with relative ease. She ascended a few meters twice and descended a few meters once, and shortly was on the opposite side of the canyon, directly above the entrance to the tunnel. On that side of the canyon, the level where Vic stood stretched upward into the mountains and was strewn with boulders and a few plants.

Vic pulled off the pack and took out the two ropes and a blanket. She kept four grenades for later and pulled out twelve for her plan. She cut three strips of blanket, each about two inches wide and eighteen inches long and then four strips as wide but a foot longer. Then she searched the slope until she secured six stout branches, each about one third meter long.

As she worked, Vic listened for sounds of worms under the ground. Since she didn't know if the worms could climb, she peered over the edge every minute or so to ensure none were creeping up the wall.

Vic put together three expedient bombs. For each she used a strip of blanket to tie four grenades along a branch. Then she ran a smaller branch through the pins of the grenades. Next she attached both ropes to a very large boulder which would easily hold her weight. Vic expected to bounce from concussion and wanted to be attached to something which wouldn't work loose. She tied the makeshift bombs to the end of one rope and lowered it slowly until the bombs were just above the entrance of the tunnel. There was still rope left so she tied a butterfly knot with a large loop to take up the slack. Then she measured out enough of the other rope to put her at the top edge of the tunnel beside the grenade bombs.

Forty-five minutes after they rode away from the canyon at full gallop, Lin and Chu arrived at the river and dismounted to let their horses rest and drink. Both were tired and there was little talk. Finally Lin stood up and looked across the dunes at the mountains in the distance. "Vic was up to something. She could have come with us, we could have ridden to find another horse. She has a plan and it must be dangerous and she wanted us safe. It's probably three hours until dark. Chu, go back to your family. Vic and I will find our way," and she mounted her horse.

"Wait! What are you talking about?"

"Vic is planning something and she might need

help. I've gotta go back, Chu. You don't. You have that great family to take care of."

"Don't get melodramatic, Lin," said Chu. "If you go, I go. You have become my friends, and even if you weren't, I am your guide. Professional pride dictates I go. Besides, I promised my friend Lao, I would protect his little cousin."

"You really think I need protection?"

"Not really." Chu let go of Lin's reins and mounted his horse. "I'll just follow and take notes."

Lin looked at him and said, "Thanks Chu. I've gotta talk to Lao about calling me his little cousin, but he does pick good friends." Then she spurred her horse forward.

The horses were tired so it took longer to return, about an hour. The mouth of the canyon was still 400 meters away when Lin said, "I swear I see Vic's pack up on the rock where she stood when we left her. I should never have gone. Do you see it?"

Chu answered yes he saw it, then pointed right. "There are some Red Beard horses in the shade of the hills." Then they heard an explosion.

"That was a grenade, I think," said Chu. "Except it sounded too big."

The two slowed as they came nearer the mouth of the canyon. A minute after the first explosion and while they were still a hundred meters away they heard a second explosion. Then they heard a rumble and rolling explosions from deep underground.

The horses balked so they halted. "What's going on?" Lin wondered aloud. "It must be Vic. She must be in trouble."

The rumble grew louder and Lin was about to spur her horse forward when there was yet another

134

explosion, then an immediate louder rolling grumble from the direction of the canyon. Then came the big one. The final explosion threw them from their horses and knocked the horses to the ground. Before the air filled with sand and blinded them, Lin saw the right wall of the little canyon move to the left side and saw stones the size of houses fly from right to left. Then the sand forced her eyes shut. Lin and Chu both were knocked silly but didn't completely lose consciousness.

It was three minutes before Lin spoke. There was still so much sand in the air that she couldn't hold her eyes open so she spit the sand out of her mouth and just asked, "Are you here Chu? Are you OK?"

"I'm OK. You?"

They heard the horses snort and rise. Chu spoke to them in Mongolian to calm them and keep them from wandering away. A few seconds later, Lin felt the muzzle of her ride against her head and she pulled herself up to stand beside her horse. A steady wind blew and it cleared the air within a few minutes.

Where the canyon mouth once opened was a wall of rubble that made it difficult to imagine there was the entrance to a canyon right there just minutes before. Lin ran to the former entrance, but there was no longer an opening or canyon. Then she ran the direction where she saw Vic's pack. She found the pack and carbine quickly, a few meters from where they rested before. The pack was covered with sand and gravel but Lin checked inside and the camera and film seemed unharmed. Then Lin called out for Vic. She mounted her horse and rode 200 meters in either direction. Chu rode in opposition to Lin and both called out, and every few minutes they would fire a shot into the air. After a few passes, they stopped at the thirty-meter-high rubble pile which was once the canyon mouth but now was simply a section of the mountainside.

"Maybe I can climb up over there..." Lin began.

"No Lin," said Chu. "If Vic was in the canyon she's gone. If she was not in the canyon, she'll expect to find us at the camp site like we said. Even with that explosion there will be horses within two or three miles for a day or more. Or she may already be back. We could easily have passed just out of sight of each other. Lets go back and wait for her. If she doesn't show up in two days, we can return."

"Vic's OK," said Lin "I know she is. But I shouldn't have left her in the first place." Lin made a fist and slammed it against her thigh. "I shouldn't have left!" Before going, Lin took Vic's journal from her pack and tore out a page to write a note. "See you at the creek." She secured it in the carry straps and put the journal back in the pack. Chu asked, "Don't you want to take her camera and notes just in case she...", but Lin cut him off, saying "Vic will want to make notes and take a photo when she returns for her gear." So Lin and Chu rode back across the dunes to make camp and wait.

Chapter 10

Many Faces of Death

After Vic lowered the makeshift bombs, she tied the end of the other rope around her waist and descended the cliff face, careful not to dislodge rocks which might alert the worms. Three meters before the end of the rope she spotted a large worm coming up the debris toward the tunnel and stopped dead still. While she waited Vic noticed several yols, large vultures, high above. Probably the heavy scent of death attracted them, but they were not descending so perhaps they were also privy to the danger of the worms and their ooze.

It seemed forever, but finally the worm was into the tunnel and Vic lowered herself to the end of the rope. There she dangled sideways with her shoulder at the top edge of the tunnel entrance.

Vic detached one bomb from the rope. She pulled the length of blanket tied to the stick that ran through the pins to arm all the grenades at once, held her arm out full length and hurled the bomb into the tunnel. As it flew from her left hand, Vic climbed up to better avoid shrapnel and stone projectiles from the explosion. She just pulled up the third arm length when the grenades detonated. The explosion bounced her against the cliff face once and she slid back to the end of the rope, untied the second bomb, pulled the pins and chucked it into the tunnel. She made it up three arm lengths again when the second bomb went off and bounced her against the cliff. There was another explosion from deeper followed by a grumble. Vic had no idea what it might be, so she just slid down to the end of the rope and lobbed the final bomb inside.

As Vic climbed, the final bomb detonated and was promptly followed by another explosion from deeper, then a subterranean thunder began to come closer and the earth trembled. She didn't know what it was, but it could not be good, so she climbed faster. At the top, she didn't slow but jumped up, grabbed the bag, pulled the loop of the rope over the boulder and dragged the rope behind as she ran up-slope. She made it a hundred meters when another explosion forced her to stop and fight to keep her balance.

Then came the big one. Suddenly, Vic was in total silence and was senseless to physical sensation. The ground billowed the way a sheet on the clothesline ripples in a breeze. The earth lifted beneath her and tilted and just as suddenly it reversed and Vic had the sickening sensation of a sudden fall. Engulfed by hot air and dust, Vic's knees buckled from a sound so violent it made her bones vibrate! Like a flare of

138

lightning the hot memory of her final breath in a cave a thousand generations before seared Vic's brain! Then her world went black!

It took several minutes before Vic became conscious and opened her eyes. Dust still hung heavy in the air, but she could see well enough to move and the explosions and grumbles were done. Vic stood and walked slowly around in a large circle. It was evident that the area of the hill where she stood was now several feet lower than it was just moments ago. What had been a slightly convex upward slope was now the concave inside of a bowl.

Vic tried to find the way back around the canyon and quickly realized there was no canyon and no simple path back. A clutter of massive boulders and loose sand and gravel remained which would be difficult to traverse and may also still conceal live worms. The safest, surest way to go was upward and look for a way around to where the mountains rose up from the desert. She turned to leave and heard a gunshot beyond where there was once a canyon. She paused. A minute later came another gunshot. Vic listened and yearned to investigate. Was it possible Lin and Chu didn't get away and were in trouble?

As she listened to the gunshots, Vic realized she turned her head to the left toward the sound. She pressed the end of her index finger into her right ear and winced from the pain. Blood was on her finger tip. That ear drum was obviously ruptured but there was nothing much she could do. She cut a small square from her flannel shirt and folded it into an ear plug to keep the wound clean, dry and warm. If it didn't get infected it should be OK in two to three months.

Six shots were fired. Ten minutes after the last, Vic coiled the rope and stuffed it in the pack, retrieved her cap which had been blown off, and headed up the slope to search for a path to the front of the mountains and back down to the steppe.

One hundred meters above where she fell, Vic found a goat trail which ran more horizontal than vertical. She moved along the trail as quickly as she could, for there was likely no more than an hour and a half until dark and it was very cold. She wanted to retrieve her pack and bedroll for the bitter night.

Vic moved quietly. There was a chance she might not get to the desert floor and retrieve her pack before dark. So she carried the revolver in her left hand and the ax in her right and kept alert for sound of any animal with skin enough to provide cover against the deadly cold.

Vic was not disappointed. Just minutes later she rounded a turn and came face to face with a large gray-black, lone male wolf. He barred his fangs, snarled and leaned back on his haunches to leap. In that instant as the wolf prepared to attack, Vic swung the ax. It struck the wolf's head and knocked it to its fore knees. The wolf yelped, then growled and raised up. The ax caught the animal on the other side of the head and finished it. Vic dropped the pack and pulled her stone knife. She rolled the wolf over on its back and began to skin it. She did not do a clean job and laughed about how the twins would scold her if they watched this. The skin was free in a few minutes and Vic removed a hind leg and stuffed it into the pack. Next she cut into the torso for the liver. It had a thin yellow cover which Vic knew was fat. She took enough slices to fill her hand and put them under her canteen in the metal cup. Then she continued on.

Vic was on the opposite side of the mountains from the sunset, so already shadows were deepened and the temperature was dropping fast when she came to a cliff edge which overlooked the desert. She peered over the brink for a way down and saw the wall was sheer. She took the rope from the pack and dropped an end over the side and it stopped about three meters short of the ground. It might be miles before she found a better place to get down. The dunes touched the mountain and no sharp stones were apparent just below. Darkness was coming fast. The decision was made to go down and she needed to move fast because once she got off the cliff she needed enough light to shoot.

She knew her weight would stretch the rope some, the drop should be no more than two meters. Easy, if nothing went wrong. If she didn't land on her feet, it could kill her, or if there were sharp rocks just lightly covered with sand, she could break a leg and lie helpless to see if a predator or the cold would claim her first. If she couldn't retrieve her gear and couldn't find the pack she set at the canyon entrance, there was no question she would freeze to death.

However, Vic was not one to dwell on such baneful possibilities. Do what needs done and Vic needed to get down from this ledge, now. She tied the pack and skin to one end of the rope, and anchored the other end around a boulder.

Vic lowered the gear then descended and in seconds, she was at the rope-end with the pack. She slid over the gear, held to the rope at its lowest point, and pushed out from the cliff wall. She swung back toward the cliff and gave herself one more push and at the farthest point from the cliff, she let go of the rope.

It worked and Vic landed in sand. She hit hard from a meter higher than she expected, but there were no rocks and she was up on her feet immediately and whipped out her revolver. The weight of the grenades and ammo had already stopped the swing of the rope. She moved from directly beneath her gear where she could see the rope against the darkening blue-gray sky and she fired. Her third shot brought it down. Vic caught the pack and was already moving back toward the defunct canyon as she slung it on.

Minutes into the walk, Vic passed a stand of zag trees and collected an armload of dry branches. Vic didn't run or lope. She knew that under the layers of clothing she would sweat even in the frigid weather and if she became wet with sweat it would make her colder. Although she walked to minimize sweat, nevertheless, she swiftly found the former canyon mouth and Lin's note with her gear. That was a relief. She quickly transferred the ammo and remaining grenades from the confiscated pack to her own.

As a precaution against worms she hiked a couple hundred meters away from that area and found a shallow dimple into the cliff wall. It would help block the wind which had picked up to more than twenty miles per hour.

With the zag branches she built a small fire at the back of the dimple against the cliff and laid four fist sized stones in the blaze. For a quick meal she cut the wolf meat into thin strips and cooked those and the thigh bone directly in the flames until charred. She knew wolf, like jaguar, is OK to eat, but must be very well done to prevent infestation by worms or other disease.

Vic ate the blackened meat first, then cracked the thigh bone and scraped out the marrow with her knife. She just finished the quick meal when the snow began. Briefly she warmed her hands over the dying flames and pulled on her gloves to set up her pup tent. Inside, she lay the sheep skin down for ground cover, wrapped herself in the MacIntosh blanket with the four hot stones and covered her head and upper body with the wolf skin. Vic guessed it to be near zero Fahrenheit and the wind chill magnified that bitter temperature. She shivered a bit but quickly warmed and fell asleep.

About two in the morning, Vic was half awake, aware that the wind was now very strong. It howled through rocks and whipped up the edges of the little tent and slipped inside to flap the wolf skin and even the verge of the sheep skin beneath her. She just thought how glad she was to not be in the open when a powerful gust pulled the tent pegs out on the side hit by the wind and she was suddenly lying in the open, holding tight to the wolf skin. The tent, still staked by three pegs, flapped hard and loud and Vic knew it could be uprooted completely and gone any moment. It was no longer snowing, but a thin sheet of ice-snow carpeted the ground.

143

The wind was strong. Her pack now held the camera and film, plus the grenades and ammunition she collected and still the wind moved it several meters. So before anything else Vic found a stone that weighed a good fifty pounds and laid it on the tent to keep from losing it.

The temperature was undoubtedly sub-zero and the wind howled at forty miles per hour! Even if she didn't mind sitting in the open, if she tried the blood would turn to ice in her veins!

She took hasty stock of what needed to be done in the situation and went to work. As she labored against the raging, frigid gale, she reminded herself that the situation could be worse and felt grateful that she was not out on the dunes fighting the full force of the tempest and that Narakaa helped them make deels.

Against the unrelenting wind Vic used her ax to chop a crater of about one cubic foot at the opening to the tent. She broke the remaining zag limbs into a size to fit in the hole. She took the wolf fat from the canteen cup and rubbed it over the largest of the branches. The fat would help a fire catch and continue and location in the crater would help protect it. When a little blaze was secure, Vic dropped four fist sized stones in the fire as before.

The wind and slippery ground made it difficult to work. Her fingers were beginning to feel over-sized and stiff from the cold which made it a challenge to use her hands. Part of her thought a break would be good, but she shivered constantly and it grew worse by the minute so she knew she couldn't rest. She needed a shelter, fast!

Vic used another stone to hammer the loose stakes into the ground but did not make the tent taut. She left it just slack enough that she could lay heavy rocks on the edge of the canvas. Then she pushed her pack inside the tent.

At last, and none too soon, she was able to snap the tent entrance and roll into the MacIntosh material with hot rocks again. Immediately, she could feel her body begin to recover.

Before slumber took her, she understood why Chu said you can hear the banshees of hell in a wind storm. It was like the wailing of the old women if a hunt for Glu, the mammoth, went wrong and many men were trampled to death or mangled. Even though Vic knew it was the wind and there was no more Glu, her ears would not let her hear anything but wailing. After an hour the wind diminished, the wails faded and Vic drifted into a sound sleep and walked in thick humid warmth beside the Restless Sea, hand in hand with Nu.

Vic managed two hours of sleep and the sun was up when she awoke. She unwrapped from the MacIntosh and shook off the fine layer of cold wet sand that managed to get inside the tent.

Then she considered her next action. She had no water and was thirsty. There was no food but she wasn't too hungry after the wolf last night. It took 45 minutes on horseback at a gallop to get to the point where she planned to meet Lin and Chu. It isn't easy to walk in sand. Vic figured it would take all day if she attempted to walk. The best plan seemed to be walk along the mountain and look for a horse.

145

Vic packed her tent, threw on her pack and began her hike. In the early afternoon, she found her horse grazing and making his way slowly back toward the former canyon. She retraced her path to the site of the closed canyon and turned across the els. It was a rough two days for both Vic and the horse and they needed water, so she didn't push. She came to the edge of the els and stopped at the river to drink an hour before sunset.

Lin and Chu saw Vic at the river and ran out to meet her. They all had stories to tell and shared them as they sat around a small fire and ate maral steak. "You should have seen Lin," said Chu. "When we returned, four maral were drinking at the river. They saw us and bolted, but Lin rode after them and very quickly brought down the largest with a shot from the saddle!" Vic thought that was fantastic and bragged on Lin's shooting and thanked her for the meal.

Lin and Chu were both curious, "What was that big explosion?"

"I'm not positive. I'm no geologist, but I have an idea," Vic told them and took another bite of the maral.

Said Lin "It looked like the whole danged mountain exploded. I saw rocks bigger than my house flying!"

Vic finished chewing the maral. "OK. I read that the oil they get out of the ground to make gasoline for automobiles, not only will burn but sometimes has deposits of explosive gas around it. It's the gas in the modern stoves and like my house lamps. My guess is that Mongolia is situated over oil and explosive gas deposits. The first two grenade bombs opened a

146

fissure to such a deposit so gas began to leak upward and the third bomb caused the gas to explode.

"I think I was on a very large rock, perhaps 200 meters in diameter. Probably it weighed at least tens of thousands of tons. When the gas exploded, like the lid on a pan of stew boiling over, the rock lid lifted and the the stuff inside went out the path of least resistance into the canyon, and the lid fell into the hollow it left. One thing is for sure, maps of that area need to be redrawn."

"That sounds exciting! Just think of what happened and you were on top of it and you're still alive," said Lin.

"That's the part I like," said Vic. "I'm still alive. If I was offered a choice I would have been far, far away when it blew."

Vic divvied up the Red Beard ammo with Lin and Chu, wrote by firelight in her journal for a time, and then climbed into her pup tent. She rolled into the skins, grateful for the delicious meat, for warmth and for a gentler wind.

VIC: MONGOL

Chapter 11

Lost Species

On waking, Chu began a fire and they drank coffee and tsai as they recounted the past three days. Then Chu turned pensive and after a sigh said, "I have fought for my life beside the two of you. You have shared a personal secret, Vic. Lao spoke of Lin with nothing but praise. I feel you are both above reproach and honorable. I wish to share a secret that you must never share and then I would ask a favor."

"What is it?" Lin asked. "You look intense. Yes, we have fought side by side and I say yes to the favor even before I know it."

Vic told Chu, "I, too, can say yes to your favor. You have shown yourself to be honorable, so I know a favor you ask will be honorable, as well.

"First let me share the secret. Show it to you. Then I will ask the favor. The favor will not seem so fantastic once you have seen the secret." Chu told them he could show the secret at the next sunrise if they rode hard all that day. So they immediately doused the fire, threw on their packs and were off. They traveled at a rapid pace and only twice did they pause a few minutes to eat aaruul and water the horses.

"I believe we will make it," Chu told them two hours before dark. They traveled along the edge of the dunes and stopped in front of a distinctive set of rocks. A four-meters-high blade of stone rose from the sand like a giant sword and immediately behind it was an almost perfectly round stone about a meter in diameter.

Chu pointed toward mountains beyond the barren sand. "The els are narrowed again at this point and those mountains are only five or six kilometers." Then he brought to their attention a mountain in the distance that looked like the pinnacle of a roof with eaves that trailed off to either side. "As the sun sets, that formation will cast a shadow spear tip to point our destination. We must reach the edge of the els below the tip of the shadow spear head before dark," he told them. "Otherwise we will need to wait another day."

They pushed hard and the horses were slick with sweat when they reached the far side of the els. It was good they did for they just had time to mark the tip of the transient spearhead before the sun and shadow disappeared.

"In the morning, I will show you," said Chu but didn't explain. They made a small fire and ate more maral before they turned in.

The daytime temperature might now warm to ten degrees Fahrenheit in the sun, but nights and in the shade were well below zero. "I hope we don't get another wind storm tonight," said Vic as she set up the pup tent. "I thought I would fly away like Dorothy and Toto the other night!"

The night was calm and once they crawled into their tents and wrapped up no one ventured out again until morning.

It was still dark when Chu called to Vic and Lin. They crawled out of their pups and found Chu had water heated for tsai and coffee. In the east, the black sky was just lightening to dark blue with golden streaks to announce the imminent sunrise. Vic and Lin sat by the fire with Chu and he told them, "We can find it now but it may not be easy."

"What is it Chu?" asked Lin. "You really have my curiosity up! Is it treasure?" Lin joked and Vic smiled.

Chu laughed and nodded, "Yes, there is a treasure and I'm sure it is bigger than I can imagine!"

"You're kidding!" Lin said.

"He sounds serious," said Vic.

Lin asked, "What is it Chu? Is it diamonds, gold doubloons or what? Are you serious?"

"Well, I saw what I think was gold, and it is in a buried castle, and any castle should have treasure in it, shouldn't it?"

Vic made another cup of coffee and Chu and Lin each got more tsai. Then Chu told the story.

Beneath the sand, very near where they sat, was an ancient castle, perhaps an entire city, covered by the sands for who knows how long. Chu first found it accidentally, many years ago in his teens. He mentioned it to a few people over the years but they thought he was joking, so now he kept it to himself

151

Without the sun pointer he could not have found the city again, for every year the els advanced nearer the cliffs and covered the city deeper. "Even knowing it is here, it may be difficult to find, but we need to do so before it is so far beneath the sands that it cannot be uncovered. It is good you came this season. The sun's movements make positioning of the pointer accurate for only a few weeks each year."

"I have visited several times so I could remember how to find it, but inside, I only ventured beyond the first room one time. I was alone and without adequate light. I needed someone to watch my back but never came near with anyone I trusted."

"Why did you need someone to watch your back?" Lin asked. "It's a buried city, so it isn't very likely someone is there to stop you."

"When I was in the room where I saw the gold I heard something like padded footsteps and I hurried back out. Maybe no person is there but after what we have seen, it may be worse."

"Maybe worms," said Vic. "Now we can watch each other's back, and even if there is no treasure, it will be exciting to explore a lost city! Do you know what city it is or anything about it?"

"No. I have asked many people who know the area if there was ever a city here in the desert. They all say no."

Chu knew the entrance to be directly out from the point of the shadow. "On my last visit two years ago the entrance was 230 paces from the edge of the sand. There was, at that time, a rift in the steppe, from an ancient earthquake no doubt, six meters long and two deep. It was parallel to and about three meters out from the edge of the els. The rift is no longer visible so the els have advanced at least 3 meters, maybe more."

"I'm excited! Let's get going!" said Lin.

Just as the sun crested the mountain, Chu walked with slightly exaggerated steps in a straight line from the mark they made. Vic and Lin were at his heels for 250 paces. Then Chu turned and looked up at the mountain. "Not quite right," he said and went another ten paces. He looked toward the mountains again, then took two more paces backwards.

"This is it!" he said and motioned for them to stand by him. He pointed to a glint at the crest of the rooftop-shaped mountain, like a mirror might make. "You need to see that glint and you can only see it for about the first half hour after sunrise. When you see it you are over or very nearly over the entrance."

The work frustrated them. As they would pull sand out of a hole, more would slide down the side. The only utensils available were zag limbs retrieved from the steppe and their canteen cups, plus they made use of the tents. Two in the hole would use canteen cups to scoop sand and make a pile on a tent, then gather up the edges and hand it up. The one up top would drag the load several feet away and dump it. Their one bit of luck was the wind. There was almost none and that helped.

They began work before seven in the morning and it was mid-afternoon when they hit the first stone. Their enthusiasm re-blossomed and they quickly located a breach in the stone as Chu expected. It was perfectly round and about three quarters of a meter in diameter. They extended the excavation to be about a third of a meter deeper than the lowest edge of the outlet, and a full meter from either side. It was late afternoon by then so they decided to wait until morning to go inside.

What they referred to as a window gathered more sand during the night, but it was quickly scooped out and in the light they could see the opening was no simple hole or window. It was more like a chute that angled down. "How long is this thing?" Vic asked Chu. He answered it was two or three meters long and round all the way. Vic had no idea what to call it, but didn't think it was a window.

Before he slid into the tube Chu confused Vic more. "Oh, be careful. There may be some glass still in the tube. It was full of broken glass the first time I came in."

Then, armed with revolvers and equipped with empty packs and haversacks and their electric lights, and of course Vic with her ax and knife, they entered the tube, first Chu, then Vic, then Lin. At the end of the tube, Lin and Chu shined their lights around. Vic focused on the large amount of rubble on the floor beside the tube and picked some up and dusted it off. In a second she shined her light through it and said simply, "Oh."

"What?" asked Lin.

"This is not ordinary glass. This is fine quality optical glass," Vic answered and slipped a small shard into a pocket.

Then Vic shined her light at the wall and wiped it with her hand. It revealed a worn tapestry and she could tell there were dust covered tapestries on all the walls. "I'd like to get a good look at this design," Vic told them. "I want to dust this off good and take a closer look before we leave, but right now lets go where you think there is treasure."

The lone door-less exit from the room opened into a tunnel which faded into utter darkness in both directions. Chu led them right and they descended for about a minute to a door which took them down a much longer set of steps inside another narrow, tunneled stairwell until they came to another intersection. Chu again led them right, again for about a minute before he paused at another opening and said, "I hope you don't fear heights."

They followed him through the doorway and found themselves on a stone platform a good thirty meters above the next floor. One-meter-wide, rail-less stone steps angled down.

"I don't like heights," Lin told Chu. "Let's keep moving."

Chu warned them, "In many places the steps have crumbled and cracked. Chu pointed at a group of foot diameter stones at the head of the steps. "There are loose stones which fell from the ceiling, too. Take care where you step."

"I've noticed damage everywhere," noted Vic.

"Maybe an earthquake destroyed this place," Lin suggested.

At the bottom they found themselves in a huge square room at least 50 meters on a side. Their lights scarcely illuminated the walls.

"Over here," Chu said and went left from the steps. He shined his light ahead and they saw where he was going. In one corner of the room was a dais raised a meter above the rest of the room. As they neared it, their lights revealed a very conspicuous high-backed stone chair in the center. They rushed onto the dais and Vic ran her hand over strange symbols carved into the stone chair back.

"This is superb work!" Vic said, "This must be a throne and we must be in a throne room! Do either of you recognize any of these symbols?"

Neither had a clue and Lin said excitedly, "If this is a throne room, this really must be a castle and there may be a real treasure!"

"Back here," Chu told them and led the way behind the throne through another doorway. It was a short corridor which led to a large circular room with an arc of six doors opposite them. "I only went in the first door on the right," said Chu. "That is where I saw the gold." So they went to the first door.

Vic and Lin both gasped when they entered and shined their lights around the room. The dazzling reflections were almost blinding! It was a narrow room but at least twenty meters deep and three walls were lined with stone tables and all the tables were laden with gold - ingots, plates, goblets, bowls, jewelry. Vic and Lin were stunned and stood in silence for a moment.

"It really is a treasure," Lin whispered.

"And what a treasure," said Vic.

They paced the room to examine the trove, but their awe did not lessen, especially when they realized that more golden treasure sat below the tables. After a few minutes, Chu spoke. "Now for the favor," he said.

"Yes, tell us," said Vic.

Chu wanted their help to take some of the treasure out, as much as they could carry, and he wanted them to take it to the United States and invest it, and on a regular schedule send funds back to Mongolia. Chu wanted to build a school for the twins and their friends who lived in the area. "It will take years, perhaps decades, before the government will build schools out here. I want my daughters to have an education. I want them to have a life somewhere besides on the steppes or in the mountains. This has been a good life but the future will be in cities and will be for those who are educated. They are naturally intelligent girls. With education they can be whatever they decide. I want them to have choices. If they choose to live as their parents, I will not be sad, but if they must live as Narakaa and I without choice, then I think I will fail as their father. Will you help me?"

In unison Vic and Lin answered, "Of course!"

In a few minutes, however, came the first snag. "Gold is heavy," Lin said. "I don't know if this will work. A pack filled only to a third will be a good hundred pounds on each of our backs. That will be a small fortune, but will it be enough to build and run a school for years? And wouldn't we rouse suspicion if we go back through the wall or board a ship bent over from the weight of our packs?"

"Lin is right," Vic said. The three sat on stone stools and looked at one another.

Chu looked discouraged, "What can we do?"

They were silent for a few moments then Vic made a suggestion. They could take out several loads, over multiple days if necessary, and cache

157

it somewhere they would be able to get to it easily in case the castle became inaccessible. She and Lin would take some now, and two or three times a year Chu could ship more, maybe with herbs to Lin's parents.

There were problems with the plan, but the problems would come later, and in the end none had a better idea right then, so they began to pack gold items into their packs and haversacks.

Lin filled hers first and said, "I'm going to take a look in one of the other rooms."

Vic said, "Stay alert."

"I'll just be in the next room. Room two." She patted her revolver and said "My friend is going with me."

Vic watched Lin go out and smiled. *Now I know how Barney felt in Africa when he thought my actions were risky.*

Lin was gone barely a minute when she called out, "Vic! Chu! Come here!"

Vic and Chu ran to the next room, each with a light in one hand and revolver in the other hand.

Lin was on her knees in front of an urn, light in one hand, her other hand full of red stones. "I think these might be rubies," Lin told them.

Vic took one and couldn't help her admiring smile. The stones were natural, uncut, but were breathtaking in their clarity and brilliance!

Chu reached into another urn and pulled out a handful of green stones. "Emeralds!" He then reached into another urn and pulled out diamonds.

"Gold in one room, gems in this room. What do you think are in the other rooms?" Lin asked.

"Let's not get crazy," said Vic. "First things

first. This solves our problem, and remember Chu thought he heard something down here before. We may need to leave in a hurry so let's dump the gold, and fill our packs and bags with gems. Then we can look in the other rooms to satisfy our curiosity."

In less than fifteen minutes they were about done and Lin finished first again and said, "I'm going to room three."

"Be careful," said Chu. "We have made a lot of noise. If something is down here, we have probably alerted it."

Lin left for room three. A couple of minutes later Vic was done and pulled her pack and haversack on. Chu just closed the straps on his pack when he saw Vic stiffen and look toward the door. He started to speak but Vic held up a hand to stop him. The hair on her neck rose and a chill ran down her back.

Chu stood and pulled his pack on. Vic kept her eyes on the door and stepped closer to Chu and whispered, "I'm sure I heard something. And my nose….there is something!"

Suddenly Lin cried out, "Vic! Chu! Watch out!"

Vic vaulted to the door and leapt through with Chu behind her, both with revolvers drawn again. They did not expect what they saw.

Standing at the next door was a man-like creature! It appeared very solid with a height about that of Vic at five feet nine inches. It was well muscled, but especially the forearms. Compared to a standard man they were quite exaggerated, with almost twice the circumference of the upper arms. Those extraordinary forearms ended at hands

159

fully as unusual - large, with defined musculature and each finger ended with a dense, slightly curved claw. The entire body including the face was covered with short sandy hair, fine like duck down. The large eyes implied a creature that needed to see in the dark, like an owl or marmoset. The head hair was the color of the body hair and hung below his shoulders, all toward the back, which left the ears uncovered, perhaps to aid in hearing. Since the thing wore no clothing it was obvious that it was indeed a male and in that respect looked human also.

When their lights hit him, the man half turned and looked at Vic and Chu and narrowed his eyes.

"You OK, Lin?" Vic called.

"I'm OK. Got light and gun both on this thing."

"Can you talk? Are you a man?" Vic asked. "Speak in Chinese and Mongolian, Chu. See if it understands." Before Chu could begin the man turned toward them, growled and stepped forward. Immediately Vic stuffed the revolver in her pants and pulled out the ax. Instantly, the man stopped and glared at Vic. "Try not to use guns. They're too loud. We need to assume there are more of these fellas around but maybe they don't know we're here, yet."

It looked intently at the ax and Vic. "An ax has been a weapon for ages. Since long before it was an implement to cut trees it was used to kill the enemy whether man or beast. "

"That means it is intelligent if it recognizes a weapon," said Lin.

Chu said, "I'm pretty sure it's a man, just a little odd. He seems to be listening."

"There is no possible way for him to know

English," said Lin, and she spoke in Chinese. The thing seemed to recognize she was trying to communicate but shook its head and grunted.

Vic spoke to him in the language of the apes and early man, but there was no recognition.

Chu spoke in Mongolian simply saying "We are friendly." The thing craned his neck toward them and emitted something like an "ah". Then it spoke. The sound was not identical to the sound of Chu, but was similar.

"He understands!" said Chu. "The words are not exactly the same. He uses words which were once common, but are seldom used now. His accent and tones are different, but close enough I think I understand." Then Chu spoke again in Mongolian and the thing answered him. For several minutes, Chu spoke with the hairy man and from time to time he translated. At one point, the hairy man pointed to Vic and Lin and spoke. Chu told them the man said they smell like women, but carry weapons, and Vic in particular handled the war ax like a warrior. Then he asked if Vic was a demon. Lin couldn't help herself and laughed out loud at that. "My friend the demon woman!"

Chu continued to speak with the man and relayed the story to Vic and Lin. His people lived deeper and they were many. They came from another world long ago, a world where a fire was always above them, and invisible forces which moved the surface they walked on into the air so they could not see, and it was sometimes necessary to wrap yourself in extra skin to keep from dying.

"Sounds like the surface with a sun and hot and cold days," commented Vic.

161

"And sand storms," added Lin.

Then long long ago the gods decided to protect them. The world trembled and roared. The floor of the world opened and the city sank and the sand covered their city to protect them from the demons roamed that world and they lived in this safe world since that time.

Chu translated, "So they didn't consider the earthquake a disaster, but a gift from their gods. I gather that not often does anyone come up where we are. I believe it was once the palace, where the ruler lived, and now it's like a sacred place. I think he said he smelled us and came to check."

After more conversation, Chu said, " I think they have been here very long. I mentioned Temujin or Chinggis Khaan, and he didn't know what I talked about. He never heard of Modu and the Xiongnu, either, who were here about 200 years BC.

Vic shook her head. "I think they have been down here much longer than that. It might take ages for their eyes and nails to change to how they are, unless they are a separate species, a lost race of man. Even that begs the question though - how does he know Mongolian, even an archaic form? He didn't mention any names familiar to you?"

"No. He said his people were attacked often by wild people who lived in the rocks and demons in the sky threw fire at them. That's why they were glad the gods put them underground."

"How do they survive?" Vic asked.

Chu asked the man, and after a minute of talk and gestures, he had an answer - mushrooms and an underground river which abounded in fish.

After another lengthy conversation, Chu grew solemn and said, "I asked how it is they don't run out of space. He says there home is very large, but if their numbers grow too many, the old are cut up and used to feed fish."

"Oh, my!" Lin said quietly. "Then they don't have emotions like compassion or remorse, at least not the same as ours."

"Everything is for the tribe," said Vic. "They are very primitive. That behavior indicates they may not even have self-awareness."

Chu had more. "He is quite upset that we are here. This is a forbidden region, a buffer to the evil world above. He keeps asking if you are a demon, or a wild person from the rocks, Vic. I don't think he likes you."

Chu apologized for their intrusion, explaining they were unaware it was a forbidden place and they would leave right away. The hairy man was puzzled about how a demon could be ignorant of a forbidden place and when Chu translated, Lin laughed again and Vic called, "You are too easily amused, Lin."

Then the man told Chu he would call more of his people to help. When Chu translated, Vic quickly said, "No! I think we need to get out of here! He seems to be done talking. Tell him we need to speak with our friend. Lin come out, don't take your eyes off our friend and join us."

Chu spoke with the man to keep his attention while Lin eased out.

"Tell him we will go now and we don't need help," Vic told Chu.

The strange man became belligerent, and

163

raised his voice after Chu told him they would go. "He wants us to wait," Chu translated.

Suddenly Vic looked behind them and said soberly, "We need to go right now!" She backed toward the doorway to the throne room.

"What is it?" Lin asked as she and Chu moved with Vic.

"I have that feeling." Vic tilted her head back as she went out into the throne room. "I smell them. More are coming!"

The man followed them. They dismounted the dais and walked quickly toward the stairway up. Alternately they watched the man and the many dimly visible doors around the huge room. The nearer they came to the stairway the louder the man became. When they started up the stone steps he roared and waved his arms wildly!

Chu said "He is warning us not to go higher."

"Why? Is this a more forbidden, forbidden place?" Lin asked but they didn't slow. They were twenty feet up when the subterranean man roared more like a lion than a man and charged after them. It was immediately obvious that he could move faster than they could as he bounded up three or four steps at a time!

"You're right Lin. We are going to a place more forbidden. We're going higher, and he must fear we will breach the barrier that protects them," Vic said as she turned to face the man.

An aggressor, no matter the size, ferocity, or power, is in a weaker position when one foot is off the ground. Vic grasped her ax at the end and below the head as the creature leaped. With all her power she drove the side of the handle against

164

the man's face. He had no feet on the ground and Vic's strength and his weight sent him over the edge of the stairs, but his giant, clawed hand wrenched the ax from Vic's grasp and it toppled to the floor with him!

At that same time the howls of several more of the underground dwellers could be heard drawing near. Vic didn't hesitate. She dropped the twenty feet to the stone floor. The ax lay on the floor beside the man. Vic grabbed the ax and clobbered the man in the back of the head with the handle. He fell forward and Vic was on her way back up the steps as a half dozen more of the men rushed in through a doorway across the throne room!

Lin and Chu were waiting at the top of the stairs and Lin had her pistol out.

"Avoid shooting them if you can, Lin. Run! I'm right behind and only one at a time can go up the tube!" Vic was half way up the steps as Lin and Chu rushed into the first hallway and ran! By the time Vic reached the top the entire horde was halfway up so she stopped long enough to lift a loose stone and hurled it down. The creature in the lead batted it aside but another stone was just behind and hit the leading man in the chest and he stepped back, tripped on another and the entire group tumbled down the steps or plunged over the side!

Vic sprinted!

Back at the tube, Lin hesitated but Chu agreed with Vic. "We can't all go up at once! Go! I'll wait until I hear Vic!" Lin hurried up the tube and pulled her pack and Chu's with her. Chu

165

waited. In seconds he heard running beyond the door and called out. It was Vic so he went up.

Lin and Chu were out when Vic reached the tube. She slipped her pack off and pushed it up the tube an arm's length and went in after it. She could hear the men outside the door!

Vic pushed up the tube once and pushed the pack. She felt someone drag the pack out and started to push herself up again when a huge hand grabbed both her ankles and pulled! Vic cried out, and tried to pull herself upward, but she was no match for the strength of the man.

The subterranean man yanked once and suddenly, from the waist down, Vic was back inside the room! Beyond the man who held her Vic saw several more. She didn't want to hurt them. They were not just wild beasts. Or were they?

The thing released her ankles and reached up for her and as it did the mouth opened wide. Vic didn't doubt. He was about to bite her and it wouldn't be pleasant! In a blur she pulled the stone knife, drove it through a hand and back out! The thing howled and stumbled back.

Vic quickly pulled her feet and pushed up the tube and then again! She pushed again as she reached above her. She felt hands on both arms and was wrenched roughly from the tube.

"Let's get away from this hole," Vic said as she stood up and returned the knife to her belt. "If they are all his size, they are too thick to pursue us but they may have crossbows, guns or just throw things."

They crawled out of the trench and lay against their packs to catch their breath.

"Holy crap, Vic! That was close!" Lin said.

"It felt closer than close down there." Vic pulled her trouser legs up and unlaced her boots to look at her ankles. Bruises were already evident all around, on the outside of her ankles from the man's hands and inside where her ankle bones were pressed together with great force.

After a few minutes, Vic suggested, "Let's cover this. I don't think we'll be going back in."

"I know I'm not," said Lin.

"Maybe next year," said Chu.

They covered the hole much faster than they dug it and there was still an hour of light when they finished. On the hard earth at the base of the mountain they re-erected their pup tents in a triangle configuration. The wind was up a bit, but they were able to kindle a small fire in the center of the tents to heat water for tsai to drink with dried maral.

As they ate they admired the treasure and it now stunned them how much they brought out. No pack was more than a quarter filled when they entered the buried city, but now all were stuffed to capacity with precious stones and pearls. Lin and Chu's haversacks held only a handful of ammunition each when they began, and with the four remaining grenades, Vic's held but slightly more. Now all three haversacks also bulged with treasure. They estimated that each carried a good twenty kilograms of treasure.

None had experience with gems but they all imagined there was ample value to have a fine school set up in the far reaches of Mongolia and much, much more!

"What was in that next room, Lin?" Chu asked.

"Silver. Just like the room of gold, ingots, goblets, everything, except it was silver. I wonder what was in the other three rooms." Lin pondered.

"Could be anything," said Chu. "What was valuable two thousand years ago?"

"It could have been incense and perfumes," said Lin.

"Or salt and tsai," Vic said. "They were probably valuable then as now."

"Or medicinal herbs," said Lin and her eyes got wide. "Unknown cures for diseases!"

"Or scrolls with lost knowledge of things we can't imagine!" Chu said.

"What do you think, Vic?" Lin asked.

"I think I don't want to think. We could drive ourselves nuts pondering what eluded us. I am frustrated enough that I didn't get to better inspect the room where we entered."

"Why?" Chu asked.

Lin said, "Yeah, what do you think was there?"

Vic answered, "I am pretty sure the dusty tapestries were star charts and I would love to have brought one."

Lin and Chu were both intrigued and Vic continued, "I'd bet a case of Cracker Jack and all the coffee trees in my hothouse, that the room was a planetarium, and the tube was the remains of a large telescope unlike anything we suppose existed long ago. If I deemed to work as an astronomer, I dare say that a lifetime career could be based on the contents of that room."

"Holy cow, Vic! Do you want to ..." Lin began.

"No!" Vic cut her off. "I don't want to go back. I'm a travel writer with an ulterior motive that has nothing to do with astronomy."

"For now at least, it would be too dangerous," said Chu. "Maybe later."

Talk did not continue long. It was below zero with a little wind and they were all glad to crawl into their tents and get warm.

Sleep came quickly and soon Vic found herself leaned against a fallen tree near the edge of the Restless Sea where she relished the warmth of the ancient equatorial sun. Then Nat-ul startled her, "Vic!"

Vic jumped up and faced Nat-ul who stood between her and the Restless Sea. "What is wrong with you? You were nearly killed! Why were you so careless?" Nat-ul's voice was that of a young girl but the words were delivered as though with a bullhorn and her anger was unmistakable. Vic never before heard Nat-ul angry, and felt herself blush. "Why do you make me ashamed, Nat-ul?"

"It is not my words but your actions that give you shame! You almost died!" Nat-ul yelled again and looked more harsh than Vic ever saw her.

"You did well to retrieve your weapon. Life is more likely to depart when you are without a weapon. Later you hesitated. Your ankles hurt do they not?"

Vic nodded.

"One more heartbeat, one more yank by the giant and you would have been in the room. You saw his teeth! He could take off a leg with a bite! One more heartbeat, and he could be feeding on your carcass! You were two heartbeats from death!"

Vic knew Nat-ul was right.

"You hesitated. You knew what to do and you

paused. In matters of life and death, mistakes will get you killed, and the gravest mistake, the cause of more death than any other, is to hesitate."

As Nat-ul spoke Vic could feel the hair rise on her neck and her senses heighten. She started to think, *this isn't real*, but stopped herself, fully aware that thought was itself hesitation. Vic trusted Nat-ul in all matters related to life and death. Nat-ul knew what it was like to face death again and again, to wage savage battle, over and over, for another day of life. Now, without conscious reason, Vic's hand went to the war ax in her belt and grasped it beneath the head.

"You know what to do in danger, Vic. You cannot have doubts. You cannot talk about it with yourself. The span of a heartbeat can mean the difference between life and death for you and sometimes for someone else, too. It should not be necessary for me to teach you the things known by children in the tribe of Nu!"

An image flashed through Vic's mind how Nat-ul - she - as a child, rushed without hesitation to battle Ur!

"Do what instinct and your heart say needs done!"

Vic's grip tightened on the war ax and she was on hyper alert. She didn't know why. Wasn't this a dream or something like a dream? Can you die in a dream?

One thing Vic surely knew, since her vision and her visit to the cave of Gr in Africa, she enjoyed a new sense that gave her a chill and made the hair rise on her neck to herald imminent danger and more than once it saved her life.

Suddenly three bodies moved as one. Nat-ul dropped and caught herself on her forearms, her face an inch above the sand!

A great gush of water fell over Nat-ul and hit Vic as a gigantic saurian rose from the Restless Sea! It hissed and the jaws sounded like a guillotine dropping as they closed on the air where Nat-ul stood an instant before!

Vic pulled the ax from her belt.

All of that happened in the same second.

The next second like a hideous water snake the saurian's head recoiled to strike again!

Vic swung the ax and it sliced a two-inch-deep gash in the front of the beast's long neck. At the far end of her swing's arc, Vic was about to power the ax back but there was no need. The wounded creature screeched and pulled into the sea.

Nat-ul was up again and they watched the beast retreat and saw the trail of blood in its wake and knew it was more sure than a dinner call. In another second, the wounded saurian thrust its head above the surface with a horrendous shriek, and the sea below the long neck became a nightmare scene of frenzied feeding! Other saurians literally ripped the doomed beast to pieces. One second more and the lifeless neck and head were pulled under and the sea was once again still.

"See how fast death can come, and how brutal it can be?" said Nat-ul. "You are strong and quick and know what to do, but if you hesitate when you must act, you will end as that creature ended."

"Thank you Nat-ul" said Vic. "I will never again endanger myself or others," she paused and smiled, "talking with myself about what to do."

"I know," said Nat-ul. "You learn very quickly." She took a few steps then stopped and looked back at Vic, "A time will be soon upon you when, if you hesitate, you will die and so will others. Do what needs done Vic, and when pain and exhaustion overwhelm you and when all your strength seems gone, call on the power of your heart."

Vic wondered at the implication of that cryptic guidance but knew it was useless to ask. She watched Nat-ul walk to the cliff side path and ascend the steep incline and enter one of the openings that she knew were the homes of the people of the tribe of Nu. She could hear laughter and people talking in the ancient language of the uprights. For a brief moment, Vic was gripped by a deep urge to again be with her people of that time, to be with Nu in that life, but the ache declined. She knew she could never ascend the cliffs either with Nat-ul or as Nat-ul, could never be with Nu in that place. That time was gone. She must find him in her new world as Vic Challenger. Then she thought, no, not as Vic. That is my name for my work. I must find Nu and be with him as Victoria Custer. I am now Victoria Custer, she spoke and it felt good to hear her own voice affirm who she was.

Vic still didn't comprehend who or what Nat-ul was. Was she simply a dream, an imagined being, a separate part of Vic's own personality, an avatar of her subconscious mind interacting with her conscious mind, a truly separate life force who dwelled inside her, or something else? Vic did come to one conclusion, however - it didn't matter. It was incredible, whatever it was. She liked Nat-ul and Nat-ul was a voice of reason and life, her counsel was always wise, and it did not matter if she had no inkling of Nat-ul's true nature.

Vic basked in the warmth of the sun for a few seconds, then felt she needed to go and she heard Lin's voice, "Vic! You plan to sleep all day? I can't believe you're not up!"

"Coming," Vic said and unrolled herself from the bedding, pulled on her dell over her shirt and trousers and crawled out into the cold, still dark morning. Overnight, there was a light fall of more ice-snow and as far as one could see, the world was under a 3 to 4 inch white cover.

From there they headed back to Chu's ger and family. For Vic there was good luck on the second day as they came around a bend onto a group of maral. She was able to pull her carbine and get a big one before they bolted. They spent the rest of the day at that spot and cut the meat of the maral, wrapped it in its skin and Vic carried it across her horse in front of her. There was no need to worry that it might spoil since the daytime temperature was now constantly zero or below.

Chapter 12

The Destroyer

They were at the point where they turned upward onto the mountain toward Chu's ger, and Narakaa and the twins, when they sighted a lone horseman racing hard toward them along the contour of the land.

"He is pushing that horse hard!" said Lin.

"No one would do that without a very good reason," Vic noted.

Chu stared intently at the rapidly approaching rider and finally spoke, "It is Ganbold. He lives further around the mountain."

The man came to them so hard that the horse almost fell as it stopped. "Chu!" Ganbold spoke in Mongolian rapidly for a moment, then turned his horse and raced off toward the steppes.

Chu's face had no color. "The Mad Baron invaded Mongolia last month and is in Urga. Burilgi, the Destroyer, one of his commanders, is here in the mountains. He is said to be as ruthless as the Baron or worse. He has burned gers and killed many. Ganbold is taking his family south and says I should do the same immediately. If the Destroyer comes there will be many, many men. He is known for overkill. It is said that he likes to wash over his enemy like a flood from the mountains," Chu told them.

"I've been washed over before," said Vic. "If he comes to fight a mother and her babies, he can't bring enough men."

"Double that," said Lin."

The three pushed their horses to a fast walk up the mountain trail in silence. With no spoken coordination, each pulled their revolver to double check it was loaded fully. "How far are we Chu?" Vic asked.

"Almost two kilometers."

All three moved their carbine from the saddle and slung it over their head and shoulder, and let it hang for quick employment.

Vic's haversack hung from the saddle and atop the gems it held grenades and cartridges for her revolver and two extra loaded magazines and loose cartridges for the carbine. Vic transferred the magazines and loose cartridges to the sash pouch of her deel. Then she slung the haversack over her head to hang on the opposite side from the carbine. Lin and Chu followed suit.

They rode on but a minute more when from the distance, from straight ahead, from higher on the mountain, from the one direction they did not want to hear it, from the direction of Chu's home, came a sound that tore at their hearts and sent a chill up their spines! Gunfire!

"Narakaa!" yelled Chu.

"The babies!" Lin shouted.

As though a single rider the three immediately galloped at full speed and spurred and whipped their horses for all they had! Abreast they rode and each in turn jumped logs and boulders as they appeared. Not one of them ever slowed for any reason and one or more constantly goaded the horses with "Choo, choo!".

Ahead, the shooting was continuous and the horses seemed to gain even more speed.

Vic flung the maral skin to the ground and loosened the war ax in her belt.

A stand of young pines came up in front of Lin and she drove her horse through them without slowing and jumped a small boulder just past them.

Then they heard new sounds - a shotgun. "Narakaa!" yelled Chu. "She lives! That is the trench gun O gave me." The trench gun sounded again and again.

Vic jumped her horse over a log.

"Narakaa is very good. but she is alone with our babies!" Fear was obvious in Chu's voice. As one, the three horses hurdled a dry rivulet.

A plan is helpful. Knowing the situation is advantageous. There are times though when you have neither, but something must be done, something that pulls at your heart and your humanity and whatever more majestic, unnamed things lie even deeper inside you. The three had no plan nor did they know what awaited above, yet they never slowed, they never hesitated nor doubted, and they came to the place of the ger with no intention of dying, but to do what needed done!

When they came over the final knoll they were to the backs of two dozen men firing at the ger. Between the men and the ger, four dead Russians bore witness that Narakaa could indeed use the trench gun!

A half dozen men on foot to their left moved along the tree line to slip up to the ger from the side while attention was toward the front.

In the trees 100 meters to the right, fully three dozen or more hardened fighters were still mounted, and watched the spectacle and waited for the men on the ground to do the job.

The three raised their carbines and fired as soon as the targets were visible. Three of the men fell dead and the others turned. Before any could return fire the three carbines sounded again and three more men dropped where they stood.

They rode through the remaining men and used the carbines as clubs. Each blow sent one more of the enemy to his end and the horses crushed others. The three turned their horses in tight circles in the crowd, again and again, The horses trampled the enemy and the riders clubbed more! In intricate circles that became figure eights, they turned their horses to the right and then the left. The enemy fired wildly without effect. Within seconds, only four remained.

The mounted riders came toward them now and as the horde spread for the charge it was evident they numbered forty or so.

Lin clubbed at one of the men on one side of her and another from the opposite side swung up and hit Lin in the side of the head with the butt of his rifle. It almost knocked Lin off her horse and Vic was about to go help when Lin and her horse did an immediate and perfect roll back, and knocked down the man who hit Lin and trampled him.

The three rode toward the men at the edge of the woods and each let the carbines dangle and pulled their revolvers and fired then fired again.

They heard the trench gun twice more. Narakaa took out the last two of the men on the ground behind them.

Those enemies at the tree line died quickly and the three brought their horses to a dead stop and jumped off and took cover behind trees. Chu's well trained horses each continued a few meters then turned and waited.

As the enemy on horseback charged, every shot by Vic or Lin or Chu killed another marauder and when the enemy saw the marksmanship of the three, they dismounted and took cover.

Vic, Lin and Chu dropped their packs and found each had multiple bullet holes. Death was repeatedly stopped by the precious gems!

Vic yelled to Lin, "We can't all run out of ammunition at the same time. Reload now Lin. Both weapons. After Lin, you reload Chu. Then I will."

They were all reloaded and firing deliberately and with every shot the number of the enemy was reduced by one. Then Chu noted, "The trench gun hasn't fired."

Lin fired, and with distress in her voice, yelled"She's just waiting to see what happens Chu. Narakaa is OK, the babies are OK!"

"I think they've gone." Chu fired.

179

"Gone?" Vic asked and fired.

"We have an escape tunnel for an emergency as this." Chu fired.

Lin fired.

"Where does it go?" asked Vic and fired.

"Down the hill behind the ger. Then she will run down the mountain to a place where she can descend a cliff and hide."

"Let's get them, then" said Vic and without any discussion, they ran to the horses. All three fired, then mounted and at top speed drove boldly toward the center of the enemy line!

They let the carbines dangle and fired revolvers as they charged the two dozen remaining men. The handguns were emptied before they were past, but they kept riding.

Vic pulled the ax out and as she rode through, she swung to one side then the other and two more of the bandits' careers were ended. Lin and Chu again took their carbines from around their necks and used them as clubs.

As Lin swung at the last man she passed, he fired. Lin felt like someone kicked her in the shoulder and it burned, then it was forgotten and Lin kept on.

As they cleared the men, Chu felt a hot slap and burn against his right leg and looked down to see his trousers torn away mid thigh, and a bloody, ragged trench through his flesh an inch deep and two inches wide. Then it was forgotten.

They had a head start now and in two minutes came over a hill and saw Narakaa and the twins running. Narakaa heard the horses and turned with the trench gun ready to fire with the grit of determination on her face and murder to protect her children in her eyes. When she saw who it was, she pushed the twins in opposite directions from her and spoke to them and then nodded to the riders.

The riders didn't slow. Vic scooped up Segree, Lin took Monkkaa, and Chu pulled Narakaa to the back of his horse. Vic thought, *these girls are fearless*, and almost like a whispered echo heard Nat-ul say, *they just know what needs done and don't question.*

They continued for a minute and Vic said, "They will catch us like this," and she brought her horse beside Lin's and without slowing lifted Segree over to sit with Monkkaa in front of Lin. "Keep going. I'll find you."

"Vic, you can't," Lin began.

"Go Lin, go, go. You have two babies to protect. I know what I'm doing. Keep going! I'll use grenades to slow those animals down and buy you some time. Then I'll get away. It's what needs done, Lin! You need time! You know it."

Before they rode on, Chu told Vic, "There may be more. I did not see Burilgi."

Then Chu and his family and Lin continued hard up the mountain out of site and Vic stopped to look around.

Vic left the trail and rode up slope to her right and dismounted behind a clump of trees. She reloaded her carbine and revolver. Then she folded her haversack fly open and took out one of the grenades from the canyon of worms and looked around. Trees and underbrush were thick so there was good cover but it also limited her use of grenades. Fortune favors the bold, however, and

Vic found a spot with a straight view across the trail and on the other side of the trail was a scree slope. Vic estimated the distance and prepared to make the most important throw of her life. Then she waited.

The wait was short. The thunder of many hooves came from just out of sight. She could tell from the sound that Chu was right, there were more than she expected. When they came in sight, Vic estimated at least 100.

The numbers don't matter, Vic told herself. Chu and his family and Lin needed as much time as she could buy them. That is what needed done whether there were ten or a thousand.

Her original intent was to use the grenades to even the odds and draw what was left of the enemy to chase her, but she expected thirty, maybe forty men. There were now too many for that plan. Even if she killed a dozen and half those who remained came after her, there would be fifty or more after her friends and those were not the odds she wanted for them.

Five men rode abreast at the lead of the troop, with the one in the center just a bit ahead of the others. Even if not for his position, Vic would have recognized the Destroyer.

Burilgi, the Destroyer, was a tall man, Vic estimated a little more than two meters. He was bony, like a skeleton with cable-like muscles covered by skin. His right cheek was a sunken scar and on that eye was a black patch, probably both from a gunshot to the face at some time in his career. Even though the temperature was below freezing, the man's torso was bare save for his own

182

thick curly gray black hair, not unlike the wolf Vic killed, and it covered his chest, back and arms.

On his wrists he wore leather bands with two inch spikes. The outer seams of his pants were also lined with spikes. Across his horse, he held what at the distance looked like an elephant gun, no doubt so he could blow men in half to engender even more fear of the Destroyer. Vic was most disgusted by his belt where scalps hung in such profusion they fell over one another. Vic had only two thoughts when she saw the Destroyer: he was bad and she must kill him if she could.

When she thought the lead horsemen were about four seconds from reaching the scree slope, Vic pulled the pin on a grenade, powered it across the breach, and scurried for a new location.

Vic learned how the Destroyer earned his reputation. Burilgi saw the grenade land in the loose rock and immediately jerked the horseman nearest him from his mount, and held him as a shield. The grenade exploded and blasted rock fragments into the side of the group and killed or wounded ten or more, but the Destroyer wasn't harmed. Stones were buried in the face and chest of the human shield and Burilgi casually tossed the corpse to the ground.

The blast also caused a small rock slide that filled the trail with loose rocks and slowed the horses. To her further advantage, the men did not see Vic so they did not yet know her position nor that she was alone. They all held rifles at the ready and looked anxiously from one slope to the other. A few fired in the direction of the explosion, but the Destroyer stopped them, and then shouted something in Russian and then Mongolian, apparently to whoever threw the grenade. Vic didn't mind she didn't understand what he said.

Vic peered through brush along a new clear line of sight. Every action must account for as many as possible, as quickly as possible, so she was thankful to see a tight cluster of men. Ten riders were bunched close, and Vic mused, *these men are untrained. Ten minutes with JJ in Mexico and I learned not to bunch like that.*

Vic pulled a grenade pin and stood and aimed for the grouped horsemen. It exploded in the center of the group. Although another half dozen men were killed and as many wounded, Vic was spotted. She pulled the pin on the third grenade and lobbed it in a high arc toward the trail. It exploded a meter above the heads of the riders. It killed two more and wounded others.

Now the soldiers all fired at Vic or in her general direction. Most were still mounted but at least twenty dismounted and began to work their way up toward her. Vic's return fire was slow and deliberate, and every shot killed or wounded an enemy. Vic realized, though, that she didn't have enough ammunition to kill them all.

She pulled the last grenade from her pouch, instantly chose a location, pulled the pin and stood. She threw it and a sharp heat raked across her right arm as she ducked again!

Vic would not wait there and be swarmed over by these animals who called themselves men. She recalled the counsel of Nat-ul, do not hesitate. She must try to kill Burilgi and she was already in motion as the final grenade exploded.

Instinctively, Vic loosened the ax in her sash and made the war cry of the tribe of Nu as she ran. The cry reverberated through the frozen forest and was so vicious that every man on the hillside stopped firing for a second to look toward the sound. After sounding the war cry, Vic halted and quickly fired twice. Two men who stared upward took those shots between their eyes! Vic pulled her knife and set it between her teeth and went on the attack! She dodged from tree to tree, fired every few steps and made each shot count!

Suddenly, a man came from behind a tree and she pushed the barrel of his rifle down as he fired. She felt a kick like a mule in her belly but ignored it and grabbed the knife from her teeth, drove it into the man's throat, and ran on!

Then her carbine was empty and she used it once to club a man then dropped it and pulled her revolver with her left hand and the ax with her right. Just steps later, another man came through young pines and slashed at Vic with his fixed bayonet. Vic thought she felt the air of the bayonet close to her face as she turned sideways to avoid it. She rammed the barrel of her revolver against the man's forehead and pulled the trigger and continued to charge down the hill full throttle! Even though the temperature was near zero, Vic was soaked with perspiration and every few steps shook her head forcibly to clear the sweat from her eyes.

Seconds later, she felt a hot punch against her left shoulder and then someone slammed her in the back with a rifle butt! Vic jumped forward and spun around and shot the man through the heart. His last act was to pull the trigger again and it felt to Vic like a hot claw raked her waist. She completed a full 360 degrees spin and kept going!

Don't stop, she told herself. Don't stop! Every inch of her body was in pain, stiff or burning or throbbing or cramping from the strain! She could scarcely catch her breath, but she remembered the fight with the jaguar and how she managed to hold on and she remembered what Nat-ul said. *When your body can do no more, use the strength of your heart.* The evil below needed to die and Chu and his family and Lin needed time to live and Vic wanted to find Nu. A potent, invincible blend of love and loathing filled her heart and Vic continued the assault!

Vic was just 10 meters up slope from the trail when she heard one machine gun and then another and then what sounded like a thousand rifles from the direction of the Destroyer's arrival. It must be the enemy firing on her but until a bullet stopped her she would focus on just one thing - Burilgi.

Through the trees she saw Burilgi, still mounted, the elephant gun held with one hand as though a toy. He faced back in the direction they came and yelled to his men. Vic continued to dodge from tree to tree and suddenly burst through the last stand of brush just four meters from Burilgi. The Destroyer saw Vic and smiled as he aimed the huge gun at her head!

It was one of those moments when total focus is finely directed upon one infinitesimal point to the exclusion of all else. For the time of a single heartbeat Vic could see nothing but the index finger of the Destroyer, magnified and in slow motion, closing on the trigger of his prodigious rifle!

In the instant, the finest part of a second,

before the Destroyer fired his rifle with one hand, Vic side-stepped, and in that split second, she recognized the rifle as a Wesley Richards .577, the same rifle she used to down the charging Cape Buffalo in Africa and marveled that the man could fire it in one hand. The heat of Burilgi's missile warmed Vic's face as it passed and the massive slug toppled a tree with a six inch diameter. While the boom of the huge rifle yet reverberated Vic jumped onto a small boulder, heaved her ax with every muscle in her body and leaped after it!

Like a cat paws at a ball of yarn, Burilgi used the rifle to bat the ax to the side, but there was no time to swing it back at Vic. She hit him full body and her weight and the thrust of her jump took them off the other side of his horse.

Even as they fell, Burilgi retained strength and presence of mind to bring a knee up to catch Vic and push her over his head. The Destroyer hit the ground with a grunt as his move twirled Vic over and she landed on her back with her own grunt.

They both immediately rolled, in opposite directions and came to their feet. Keeping her eyes on the Destroyer, Vic made two hops then leaned sideways to retrieve her ax.

The Destroyer struck at her fast, with one hand then the other. It required but a few swipes for Vic to realize he wasn't trying to punch or backhand her, but merely rake her with the spikes on his wrists.

Vic dodged and backed and circled the man. She blocked his swipes with the side of her ax and when he suddenly kicked high at her face she stepped back and leaned back at the waist in one

187

move. His foot was just inches from her face and she got a clear view of the three inch metal spike embedded in the toe of his boot. His foot went down but he kicked again and again Vic stepped and leaned back to avoid his boot and spike.

Then a concerned voice sounded in Vic's mind. *Defense is death* and Vic knew what needed done. When the next kick came she didn't wait for the next but swung the ax hard and forced the Destroyer to jump back.

The man rebounded again with another kick and as it went down without contact Vic's ax swept across between them again. That pair of actions repeated again and as it was about to repeat once more, Vic stopped the arc of her blow short to back swing early. The back of the ax head clipped the Destroyer's knee and knocked him off balance. He didn't fall but hopped sideways and stumbled as Vic began another sweep.

Burilgi roared in rage and struck out with his arm. His anger caused the man to miss-time his blow, so his arm and Vic's ax met and the ax won. The man's right arm was taken off at the elbow and his forearm somersaulted to the ground!

The Destroyer bellowed like a wounded bull mammoth and swung his remaining hand at Vic again and again and all the while his blood pumped out from the amputation wound. Vic dodged and swung her ax and dodged again. Then when Burilgi kicked at her again, once more she came back with the back side of her ax head and slammed his knee. The man stumbled back and before he could regain his balance, Vic swung the ax up. The side of the ax head caught the Destroyer beneath the chin and he fell back hard.

Vic raised the ax overhead but stopped. Burilgi looked fearful as he frantically tried to reach behind him and roared oaths in Russian!

Vic kept her weapon poised but didn't strike. Within seconds the roars became histrionic screams as the man thrashed wildly and still strained to reach behind him. Then the directed reaching became uncontrolled convulsions! The great Destroyer began to belch the sauerkraut of his last meal. His eyes were wild with the fear of death which he dealt so casually to countless others. Vomit spewed from his mouth and an equal amount was sucked into his lungs.

As she watched the man die, Vic noticed the tip of the severed forearm jutted from beneath the man's shoulder and realized he was impaled by his wrist spikes.

Suddenly a pistol sounded to Vic's right rear and before she could turn a White Russian dropped to her left with a fresh bullet hole in his forehead. She looked back and gave a sigh of relief. Lin stood there with her revolver in hand.

"You OK, Vic?"

"I'm Ok, Lin." Vic breathed deep and looked toward the gunfire. "You were supposed to be away from here and safe."

"I left you at the worm place and felt like crap. Didn't want to feel that again, Vic," said Lin.

"Then let's finish this together, Lin."

"Rest Vic," Chu emerged from the tree line with Segree holding his left hand. He used his rifle as a cane in his right hand. Beside him walked

Narakaa with Monkkaa holding her right hand, and the trench gun ready in her left hand.

"Let the others finish it. You've done enough," said Chu. "Oh, don't touch those spikes, they're tipped with poison."

Vic half smiled, "Yeah, I figured that."

"We have all done enough," said Lin. "Besides, from here I see four wounds. You earned a break." Vic looked at herself and found a nick on her right arm, and a hole in her left shoulder with an exit wound in back which soaked her deel and shirt with her blood; a wound across her right waist luckily ripped through only muscle and skin, but did leak a lot of blood. Her ax stone had an inch deep impression in the center, surrounded by concentric circles where the first Russian who came from behind a tree fired at her point blank. The ax saved her.

Nor were Lin and Chu without wounds. Lin had a shoulder wound like Vic's, a bayonet slash on the opposite forearm and the right side of her face was swollen and bruised, her eye almost closed, from the rifle butt early in the battle.

Chu had a wound in his right thigh and the back of his left arm, and his deel was opened across his belly where a bayonet cut a skin deep gash across his full width and he couldn't remember when it happened.

"You said four wounds, I see only three," Vic said to Lin.

"Your cheek, Vic. You'll probably have a scar."

Vic didn't ask which side, but touched her left cheek. She felt the blood and looked at it on her fingertips and smiled her recognition. The bayonet came closer than she knew. It wasn't just the wind of the passing blade she felt!

"Who are they fighting?" Vic asked.

Ganbold who warned them of the danger was not the first to flee the mountains. Others fled a week earlier. Some went to Dalan bulag. Bayarmaa heard of the danger and knew Captain Unegen was in Gazar so went to ask his help. He was glad to give it for friendship of Chu, but to crush the Destroyer's force was the kind of exploit which could single handedly make a career, also. So the captain brought 200 of his most experienced Mongol soldiers and arrived just in time.

Captain Unegen witnessed Vic battle with the rogue Russian commander. Literally in awe, he said "That jaguar never had a chance! You are a mighty warrior!"

At that, Vic laughed and couldn't stop a brief stream of tears. When the captain asked Chu what was wrong, Vic told him she was so honored that a Mongol warrior and officer would say those things, then called the captain a hero and a treasure to Mongolia. The true reason for tears was joy, for no one had called her a mighty warrior for a thousand generations and earned recognition is a joy for anyone, even warriors and re-incarnated cave girls. Vic knew Nat-ul would look down on public show of emotion, but it was right for Victoria Custer. Her reply, of course, ensured that if Vic wanted it, she could have an escort of a thousand men for the rest of the trip, but she didn't.

Captain Unegen shook Chu's hand and told him his father would be very proud and if he wanted to join the army he would be a captain.

The captain turned to join his men and then stopped, looked back and made the perfect finale to a brutal, bloody battle. "Tell Vic Challenger's servant girl she also is a brave warrior. Even Temujin himself would feel pride to battle with these warriors!"

When the last Russian was dead, the captain told his physician to look after the wounds of Vic, Lin and Chu, but before the doctoring began Narakaa got an idea and Vic thought it was good. Narakaa retrieved Vic's pack and camera and photographs were taken of everyone in various combinations. Many included the captain and wounds were obvious in all. On his request, a full role of film was taken of Vic, and the others with the captain and the dead destroyer and given to Captain Unegen.

The captains physician was not a physician but a hardened, professional soldier with a lot of experience dressing battle wounds. He carried needles and catgut to close wounds, and antiseptic and bandages, so he more than sufficed and they were grateful.

Vic sat on a boulder beside Lin, and as the man worked on their wounds, the Captain brought her knife. She thanked him and wiped the knife with antiseptic. Then she asked, "Lin, remember that blood brother thing? There's no law that says men only. Want to be blood sisters?"

"Sure thing, Vic!"

Everyone stared wide-eyed when each pulled her knife across a palm, then clasped their bloodied hands together and spoke, "Sisters!"

Then they heard another, "Sister?" Narakaa stood there holding her stone knife. Vic and Lin didn't look at one another, for each knew what the other would say. They both nodded and Narakaa pulled her stone knife across her palm then grasped the hand of Vic and then Lin and each time said, "Sister!"

The next day before Captain Unegen and his troops took their leave, Vic presented the captain with her stone knife and saluted him and the captain returned her salute. Beside Captain Unegen rode his aide who carried a pole on which the head of the Destroyer was impaled. When he was gone, Lin said, "You were right Vic. It's his country and culture. He may seem brutal and vicious, but in his way he is a brave and honorable soldier; a patriot standing up for his country."

Chapter 13

Going Home

Vic and Lin stayed another five days at the ger to rest, but there was little of that. Much of their time was spent with the twins. They played in the snowy woods and lost shagai games and although the temperature was never above ten degrees Fahrenheit in those days, neither Vic nor Lin complained of cold.

On the third day, they remembered to retrieve the other packs and gems. Vic also found her maral skin intact and the meat for Narakaa and the twins was untouched, but Lin's camera took two bullets for her. Narakaa wanted to make them new dels because of the slashes and bullet holes, but they preferred to patch their original dels.

Chu planned to take them back to Kalgan but they defiantly refused. It would take him away from his family too long. They would simply retrace the same path they came by, avoid people, and forego a side trip to Gazar, even though they knew the captain would treat them like royalty.

Vic and Lin returned the borrowed carbines to Chu along with the unused salt, tsai, and rubles. Of course, they gave their magnifiers to Monkhaa and Segree.

When they were leaving, Vic gave the ax to Narakaa and told her through Chu, "You are incredible. You faced a hundred men to protect your babies and not once have I heard you even speak of it nor complain of the ordeal. I hope you never need this but if you do, may it serve you well. I am proud to know you Narakaa, my sister."

The twins gave Vic and Lin each a bag of sheep ankle bones and told them to practice and as Vic pulled the auto away, they held their hands up and gave Vic their version of the war cry of the tribe of Nu, told them "Bayartai", then yelled between giggles, in Mongolian, Chinese, Russian and English how much they loved nice big sister and nice girl. After the ger was out of sight and they could no longer hear the twins, they rode in silence for over an hour.

"It will be nice to get home," Lin finally said in little more than a whisper, "but I'm going to miss those little girls. I'm pretty sure, for awhile I'll be waking up ready to run out and chase them through the woods, or squat in the snow for a serious round of cat's game."

Vic said, "Well, there is no reason why we can't visit again. We should inspect the school from time to time don't you think?"

That made Lin smile big, "You're right! We will be like administrators or big donors or something. Don't even need to go for a story. Just see the school and play hide and seek!" Lin took a deep breath. "I feel better. I felt so heavy. Maybe next summer when it's warm!"

Vic laughed. "Who knows? But you will still love them Lin, no matter when it is. Like your aunt and mother after years apart. For love, time doesn't matter."

Then Lin told Vic, "I think I understand when you talk about doing what needs done. When we charged up that hill and in the middle of the enemy, all trying to kill us, I never felt afraid, but I didn't feel brave either. I just knew Monkkaa and Segree were in danger and to save them, I needed to kill as many men as I could, as fast as I could. I never felt more focused in my life."

The trip to Dalan bulag was uneventful. They timed it so they rolled into Dalan bulag in the day. When they parked at the trading post, the same five men as before loitered outside and they thought there might be trouble, but were able to enter without incident. They delivered a letter to Bayarmaa written by her granddaughters, to thank her for sending Captain Unegen.

When they were ready to go, Bayarmaa walked with them. Just out the door, the man who seemed to be the leader of the loiterers stepped in front of them and spoke to Bayarmaa who told Lin in Chinese who translated for Vic. "He wishes to tell you, that he has never seen better shooters, and he heard how you defeated the Destroyer and thanks you."

Vic and Lin both smiled at the man and said thank you in English, then Vic asked "How do you say thank you in Mongolian?" Then she and Lin both told the man " Bayarlalaa," and Vic asked Bayarmaa to tell him they were very proud to do something good for his beautiful country. He nodded and stepped out of the way. There was no smile on his lips but Vic and Lin both later swore that behind his hard expression, they saw a smile in his eyes.

Three days after Dalan bulag, they came to the wall outside Kalgan. They sold the auto back to the man Chu bought it from for half what Chu paid, which is what Chu told them to expect. Then they packed the dels and revolvers.

Chin was at the wall and recognized them and said to say hi to Lao when they saw him. To make things look on the up and up to anyone who might be watching, they opened their packs and pulled out the wolf skins and the deels to show Chin. Underneath the wolf skins, in each pack was a bag sewn from two tarbagan skins and each held five kilograms of gems, but who would want to see a marmot hide? An hour later they were on the train to Peking and Vic wound and set her watch for the first time in 70 days.

For three days they ate, rested and shopped and each night they both took a turn, a long turn, in a very hot tub of bubbles. Vic took photos of Lin with her relatives, and later back in Nebraska, Lin's mother couldn't stop crying and laughing when she saw the photo of her big sister with her eldest daughter.

They didn't have booked passage so when they took the train to Dairen, Lao went to help them get on a ship. He had friends on the docks he thought could help, but it turned out to be unnecessary.

They were at the harbor, on their way to see

someone Lao knew, when Lin punched Vic on the arm and said excitedly, "Hey look!"

The Red Dragon was there. They explained to Lao and approached the ship. The sailor at the gangplank recognized them so they said their goodbyes and thanks to Lao and went up to see Captain Chuluun.

Captain Chuluun was more than happy to take them as passengers again. Both yet wore bandages on their shoulders, and the scar, nicely healing on Vic's left cheek, was obvious, as was the bruise on Lin's face. "It looks like you ladies might have run into some trouble," Captain Chuluun said.

"Nothing we couldn't handle," said Vic.

"Just did what needed done," Lin said.

Suddenly the captain's eyes widened and he looked as though he was trying to puzzle something. Even though phones were new and not everyone owned one in China in the last month of 1920 and few people sent telegrams, somehow good news always gets around.

"Say! You two didn't have a run in with a fellow called Burilgi, did you?"

Vic was silent but Lin replied, "We sure did."

The captain refused to take their fare. Their passage was on him. They tried again and again to pay, but he wouldn't have it.

Vic and Lin were putting on the Ritz every night at dinner and wore the prettiest silk dresses they were able to find in Peking, with their wolf pelts turned stoles. There were no boring dinners for that trip. They sat with a new group each night and everyone wanted to hear about the bandages, how Vic got the scar and why Lin was bruised so badly. Their favorite question was, 'Where did you buy those nice wolf pelts?" One or both would answer, "Buy? Oh, we didn't buy these, we..." They had a lot of fun with that.

The trip was a reverse of the trip over, so a week later they were ready for Hawaii. They planned to just stay over-night and continue with the Red Dragon but Evelyn convinced them to stay. It was only a few days until Christmas, and they could not get back to Nebraska in time, so why not stay until after Christmas? Captain Chuluun gave them a name of another captain, a good friend, who could give them passage January 1st and make sure there were no problems getting everything safely ashore in San Francisco.

Vic and Lin were happy to have a vacation in Hawaii, where they wouldn't need weapons, or wake up cold, or worry about sandstorms. The day they arrived was perfectly warm and sunny.

Days were spent mostly at the beach. Nights were wild for Lin and Evelyn as they dragged Vic into games of mahjong with them, joined by Evelyn's Uncle Charlie, and his number two son and number one daughter.

Vic didn't mind the mahjong, because there was also conversation of famous cases which Charlie solved. Charlie also provided plenty of witticisms and Vic's favorite was, 'To lose is like driving very large nail in house. Make it stronger." Of course Lin couldn't resist that opening and said, "Then Vic will last forever."

On Christmas eve they attended a service at Kawaiaha'o Church with the Chan family. The church planned to serve dinner for needy families the next day and give out gifts to children, and along with the entire Chan clan they volunteered to help. Charlie helped Vic find a shop open late, and she used the last of her expense money to buy 200 little jade elephants and turtles on leather cords to give to kids the next day.

As they walked back from church the next day, Vic stopped Lin and Evelyn and faced them. The three earlier agreed not to get gifts but just spend time together, so they were surprised when Vic said, "I have something for you two."

Both Lin and Evelyn started to protest but Vic suddenly grabbed and pulled them together and said, "A great big hug. Thank you both for a magical Christmas!" Then Vic said, "I'm going to lope back to your house, Evelyn. See you there!"

Evelyn started to lope too, but Lin stopped her. "Vic always acts hard boiled, but she can get emotional, too. Personally, I think her emotions are what make her strong, but it also embarrasses her. Let her get ahead so she can lope alone."

When they passed through San Francisco, Lin convinced a Chinese language paper to publish her stories of adventure travel, so she would be doing what Vic did only in Chinese.

Vic and Lin arrived back home in Beatrice on January 12, 1921. The parents of both, and Lin's brothers and sisters, were there to meet them. Vic and Lin assured everyone they were fine, which of course no one believed when they saw the wounds.

Vic's mom told her that most men wouldn't want a wife with a scar on her face. Vic just laughed her good natured laugh and hugged her mom and said, "It's OK mom. It doesn't matter if most men wouldn't like it. Somewhere there is one who does." Vic was intrigued when her mother made a half smile and nodded knowingly.

Neither Vic nor Lin knew what she was doing so it took several weeks to go from marmot hides full of gems to cash and a business set up for the school in Mongolia. Once done, they began to wire money to Lao, who bought supplies, which Chu took by caravan from Kalgan.

Both nearly died and both had permanent scars. Their friendship grew even stronger. They made incredible new friends who regardless of distance would be a part of their lives always. Lin was filled with unbounded joy and pride that she was able to help Monkkaa and Segree. Vic felt equal pride over the same aspects of the trip as Lin, but an emptiness yet filled her heart for there was never a sense of Nu.

Two days after returning to Beatrice, Vic and Lin were having root beer floats at Mortimer's Drug and Lin thanked Vic. "That was some vacation! When do we go again?" Vic was already planning.

On the day after they arrived back in Beatrice, on January 13, 1921, Vic began to plan the next trip. She spent hours each day in the library, looking over maps of South America, Iceland, Great Britain, Australia and other places, and hoped that some extra sense would prompt her about where to travel but no place seemed to beckon more than the others. Of course, she often wondered if Ann Darrow would convince Carl Denham to share the location of Skull Island.

Vic found no clues to Nu, but she had a strong sense of something unfinished or incomplete. She experienced the same sensation following the vision in Africa when she recalled her previous life. It was a vague inkling about something lacking or unconsummated yet the identity of the something was even more vague than the sensation itself.

Wherever the future might lead, Vic knew fully there may be more danger, pain, and injury ahead, but nothing short of death would halt her quest.

True love never dies. To Victoria Custer it was a sacred commission, an inviolable commitment, to search a lifetime if needed, and face any challenge, to find her eternal love, Nu, son of Onu, who slew Gr, devourer of men and mammoths for his one true love, Nat-ul, wondrous daughter of Tha, of the tribe of Onu, that once dwelt beyond the Barren Hills beside the Restless Sea.

Things which matter most must never be at the mercy of things which matter least. - most often attributed to Goethe

You don't need to be brave. You just need to do what needs done. - Vic's Motto

The Adventures Continue...

Join the further adventures of Vic Challenger.
Visit http://www.vicplanet.com
Or Amazon, Barnes & Noble or ask your bookstore.

#1 *Vic: Time Doesn't Matter* 978-1-889823-38-6
#2 *Vic: Mongol* 978-1-889823-60-7
#3 *Vic: Never Give Up* 978-1-889823-61-4
#4 *Vic: Terror Incognita* 978-1-889823-63-8
#5 *Vic: Fast* 978-1-889823-62-1
#6 *Vic: Event* 978-1-889823-65-2
ISBN's are for paperback editions.
More to Come!

Howlers Illustrated story 978-1-889823-37-9

Vic Challenger's Incredibly Delicious Recipes for Bacon Lovers. ISBN 13: 978-1-889823-10-2

Several Vic Challenger journals are available.

Authors appreciate and need reviews. If you have a couple of minutes, some places you can leave a review are Amazon, Barnes and Noble, Goodreads or your own web site / blog.

If you enjoy Vic Challenger adventures, share the fun and tell others about them!

Want to be first to know when another Vic novel is out? Join Vic at
http://www.vicplanet.com/joinvic

Get free posters at http://www.vicplanet.com

Curious?

1. Mongolian cities have had multiple names over time. When Mongolia was autonomous, cities were named in the Mongolian language. When under influence of China or Russia, cities had different names. Vic mentions Urga, the capital. Before 1911 it was known as Khüree. It is now called Ulaanbaatar. Notice the map at the beginning of this book - Peking is now Beijing. Vic entered Inner Mongolia (actually an area of China - Mongolia was referred to a Outer Mongolia) at Kalgan which may also be referred to as Dongkou. See the Thank You to Hawaii State Librarians in the front of this book for what it took to find the earlier name of Dalanzadgad.

2. The Mad Baron (Baron Roman Nikolai Maximilian von Ungern-Sternberg) was real. He controlled the Mongolian capital for a few months in 1921. He actually had the facial wound given the Destroyer in the book.
https://en.wikipedia.org/wiki/Roman_von_Ungern-Sternberg

3. The game of Prosperity eventually became known as Monopoly.

4. Maral = wapiti = elk.

5. Cryptids - The most basic definition is a plant or animal whose existence is questionable. The Mongolian death worm has a history of sighting that goes back over a thousand years.
http://theunexplainedmysteries.com/Mongolian-death-worm.html Short video:
http://www.animalplanet.com/tv-shows/other/videos/freak-encounters-mongolian-death-worm/

In addition to bad guys Vic meets at least one cryptid on every trip. Full references with links are available at http://www.vicplanet.com

Lightning Source UK Ltd.
Milton Keynes UK
UKHW01f0616060718
325319UK00001B/20/P